Rogue's Temptation

Courtney Prohaska

Contents

1

CHAPTER 1

E lizabeth POV

I walked as quietly as I could, looking behind my shoulder every few steps. I was scared of getting caught because if I did I would be killed. The Blood Moon pack is not a fan of rogues. If they find one then the rogue is found dead, killed off by the members of the pack.

I am a rogue. I didn't ask to be one but I was never given the choice. It was my father's fault that me and my mother were rogues now. He betrayed our pack and escaped. The pack, wanting to blame someone for my father's betrayal, accused his unfortunate family of his crimes. We were forced out of the pack and since then we lived life as unwanted rogues. I was 10 when that happened. I was young and had not had the privilege of my first shift yet so it was hard for me. My mum did everything in her power to provide for me in those dire times and now I am repaying the favour.

I kept walking quietly. I came to the Blood Moon pack to steal some things we need like clothes, food and anything else I can find. It is either that or suffer with my mum. As I walked, I heard a growl coming from somewhere behind me. Acting on instinct I turned around but there no sign of a disturbance.

I took a deep breath trying to calm myself. I started to walk again, when I thought I felt someone behind me but I shook it off, believing it as paranoia. I kept on walking when suddenly something hit my head from behind. And then, everything went black.

Alex POV

I stood and watched the rogue in front of me scream in agony and pain. My grin only grew wider and I took pleasure in the man's torture. I hate rogues. If any unwanted people enter my territory, they are killed immediately after being tortured to the point of submission.

I am cruel, ruthless, bloody and I did not have any mercy. I am known as being that way through the other packs and I like it that way. I never showed any warm affections towards anyone, I stopped that when my family was killed in my presence by rogues. That is when I became cold hearted and I enjoyed the suffering and pain of all rogues.

I was about to add more pain to the rogues condition when the door suddenly opened and my beta, Drew, entered. He stopped before me and looked at the ground.

"I do not like to be disturbed," I hissed at him but he stood his ground.

"Alpha, we have caught a rogue. She stole some weapons before we caught her though we took back the weapons." He said and I was surprised. Female rogues were rare and more surprising, she dared to steal. She was asking for death.

"Where is she?" I asked through clenched teeth. I was impatient to see her. She has to be tortured so I can make her regret the decision she made to enter my territory.

"In the prison cells. She is awake now but she does not seem to be faring very well with the men watching over her," he said in a low voice.

"What do you mean?" I was now impatient to see her.

"Well, she started cursing at the people who caught her and then started threatening us," Drew told me. I could not help but laugh, she seems to be entertaining and that gave me more reasons to make her suffer little longer before her death.

"I am going to see her and I don't want anyone to interrupt me," I growled and Drew nodded quickly at me. I made my way through the cell and took one last look at the man behind me. I smirked, enjoying the pain he was in.

Elizabeth POV

I woke up an hour ago and started cursing at the men who watched over me. I am scared from the inside out but I can never show that to them. I want to go back to my mum and the other rogues who are like my family. When my mum and I were forced out of the pack, we joined a group of rogues who were also forced out of their packs, or they willingly wanted to be out of the pack because they did not want to play by the rules.

Our numbers increased and we soon became one hundred and fifty rogues in all. I know we are a huge number but any pack is larger than us so we are still at a disadvantage. I sat in the cell now, waiting for them to kill me. I am going to die before finding my mate, I chuckled at the thought. I didn't want a mate especially after my father betrayed my mother and broke her heart. She remained heart broken for years over her mate who was supposed to be her only true love, he was supposed to stay with her forever but he went and betrayed the pack and we took the blame.

I shook my head, I didn't want a mate. I am a rogue now, my life is mainly running around to anywhere I like and not to settle down on one place like a pack. I heard someone coming towards the cell and I stood up as I watched who it is.

Suddenly there was an amazing scent that floated through the air. It smelt so delicious even though I didn't know what was it. A man came and stood in front of me and I could not help but gasp. He was breathtaking. He has black messy hair, a strong jaw, and his eyes are black and deep, as if I could see into his soul.

I felt drawn to them. His eyes were full of hate and disgust, and for some reason, this hurt me but I didn't know why. I felt the power emitting from him and it was so strong that it overwhelmed me. It finally clicked. He's an alpha and what I heard about the Alpha of the Blood Moon wasn't pleasant. He killed every single rogue without mercy. Few people from my group went there and never returned. I should have seen this coming and I regret ever stepping foot in his territory.

I looked at him and that delicious smell was rolling off him in waves. Suddenly, I realized it.

"Mate."

My wolf howled with joy.

I stood frozen in my place. No this can't be happening. I don't want a mate, especially the Alpha who kills rogues and killed a few members of my group. He is a killer. I heard him take in a sharp breath and without looking, I knew he realized it too. I am depressed and was in deep thought so much so that I didn't notice him bending the bar cells, as if they were nothing.

He entered and stood in front of me, grabbing my chin, he forced me to look into his eyes.

"Mine." He growled.

I looked anywhere but at him.

"You are my mate," he said as he raised my head so I could look him in the eyes.

"Mine, Mine, Mine," he repeated looking intensely at me. His black eyes piercing through my own.

"No, I don't want you. You are a killer." I managed to say.

I regretted it a second later.

"I don't care about your opinion about me, right now you are coming with me," he growled and grabbing my elbow he forced me behind him.

"Fu-" I was about to curse at him when his hand covered my mouth, preventing me from talking. He looked at me with those eyes but now they looked sinister.

"There are a few rules here you will have to follow. One: no cursing.

Two: you are mine and only mine.

Three: you will do as I say.

And four: I don't want any man touching you other than me." His eyes turned darker now and I was scared but I did not back down.

"I don't belong to you or anyone and I will never obey you!" I said angrily.

He grabbed my elbow with more force and I'm sure that it will leave a bruise.

He lowered his head and whispered hotly in my ear, "You are lucky you are my mate because I would have killed you if you were not and for your disobedient behaviour, I will have each one from your group of rogues killed, starting with your family."

He snarled evilly down at me and I could see how serious he was.

"No, I will never belong to you!" I spluttered out as I began to shake.

Wrong thing to say ... The next thing I knew, his eyes turned darker and his teeth pierced through my skin at my neck, marking me.

It was overwhelming for me to take all of this in one day. The tears streaming down my cheeks and his breath tickling my face were the last thing I remembered before blacking out for the second time today.

2

CHAPTER 2

Elizabeth POV

I kept running as fast as I could. I was almost there. If he caught me, I do not know what I will do

"Run little kitten, run ... " His husky voice made fear creep into me and I increased my pace.

Suddenly, two arms wrapped around my waist, brought me to a halt and shoved me to a tree.

Black eyes stared into mine. " You dared to run from me and for that you need to be punished. " He whispered fiercely as he brought his lips to mine.

I woke up sweating, not knowing where I was. Shaking and in pain, I groaned. It was too much for me to handle. I brought my hand to my neck absent-mindedly and felt a mark there. I gasped.

I remembered everything now. I have found my mate who is an alpha and who hates and kills rogues like me. I remembered how I provoked him, just after he told me his rules, leading to him marking me by force.

I felt hot tears gather in my eyes but I refused to cry. If I cried then I would seem weak and I knew he wanted that seeing as I am a rogue. He would love to see me weak and broken in front of him but I would never give him the satisfaction of seeing me like that.

I looked around, noticing the king sized bed I was currently on and a large bedroom. All the furniture in it was elegant and precise.

I clenched my teeth, trying to not to feel pain. I stood up, ignoring the pain but fell to the ground. The pain was too intense, I felt like burning up. Every part of my body ached.

Just then the door opened and my mate, the alpha, walked in. Seeing me on the ground he shook his head and frowned at me.

Of course he will frown at me, I am a rogue. I didn't expect him to do anything other than that.

He knelt down in front of me and caressed my cheek but I slapped his hand away. He growled at me, his eyes turning darker, then he grabbed my face roughly and brought my head down to look at his face.

"I marked you now! You are mine, only mine, and I disapprove of the way you are treating me when I have done nothing to you!" He growled at me and I felt like I was going to cry. I felt like I was an emotional mess now.

"Marking me by force, if I may add and I do not like that," I said in a low voice.

"I am supposed to mark you when I first see you and I did just that so why are you angry?" He hissed at me.

Tears ran down my cheeks, I couldn't keep up the strong act. I wanted to leave and I couldn't stay with a man as emotionless and vile as this. A man who killed members of my group.

"Let me leave and I won't bother you again." I told him softly hoping he would understand me.

He chuckled at that. "I would never let you go, you are staying here with me." He whispered to me.

I refused to stay with someone as cold hearted as him, I would just live an unhappy life.

"I am a rogue. You hate them and kill them but are you willing to keep me?" I asked through clenched teeth, letting my anger towards him show.

"I hate them and I kill them also, you are right! I know you are a rogue but you are not a rogue any more. You are now a member of my pack." He smirked and I gasped.

I didn't want to live with him while he was killing off my group, who were like my family, I could not .

"I will stay with you if you stop killing the rogues," I said to him, trying to convince him.

"You think I would make a deal with you?" he laughed at me and I frowned.

"You are staying here and I don't care if you want to or not." he said casually as he stood up.

"Then I am leaving and you will never see me again! " I said angrily to show him that I meant it.

"Okay, go, leave. I will just catch you again." He said nonchalantly and left the room.

I sat on the ground now, tears running down my face. That was cruel. He is a cold hearted, emotionless beast who didn't care about my opinions and still will kill members of my group. An he thought that I will stay here and let him. He could never be more wrong.

I stood up, ignoring the pain as much as I could. I looked through the large window. I can jump, I could, of course, faint from the pain but I am willing to take the risk.

I took the last option and jumped on the newly trimmed grass. I stumbled and fell. Feeling dizzy, I stood up again and began to make my way through the garden. And that was when I heard it.

Someone was screaming in pain and my heart ached for the person. I wondered what or who was causing the person that pain. I had two options, either leave right now, or go and rescue whoever was screaming.

Before I could think about it, I went by option two. I could never leave anyone behind so I ran towards the sound and I found myself in front of a big room in the middle of the huge garden.

I swallowed nervously as I entered the room and the sight in front of me made me go speechless. I gasped.

A man was in front of me, hanging from the ceiling by two ropes around his wrists. I looked at his face and it was a mess but I focused more on his facial features.

He was a member of my group, I'm sure of it. He was one of our fighters and he disappeared last week. Or, at least that is what I heard.

He raised his head and looked at me he looked shocked.

"Elizabeth, is that you?" he managed to say even though he could barely move.

I nodded at him, tears filling my eyes at the sight of him. I have to get him out and I didn't care about any consequences.

I quickly ran to him and tried to reach the ropes but it was too high to reach. I grabbed a chair, stood on it and began removing the ropes.

"Elizabeth, you have to leave now! He will come and you will be just like I am now!" He said in a harsh whisper, pleading to me.

I shook my head. There is no way I am leaving this man here. I removed the ropes and he fell to the ground with a thud.

I quickly got down and brought him close to me, hugging him, trying to make him forget about the pain.

I was concentrating on the man so much that I didn't notice Alpha Alex come in, and boy, did he look scary.

He glared at me and in two quick strides, pulled me away from the man roughly.

He growled at me. I made a move towards him but he pushed me away cruelly causing me to fall down with a loud thud. I could feel my side flare from the excess pain.

I looked at Alex as he made his way towards the man, not knowing what he was about to do until I saw his claws extend.

It happened so fast, that before I could open my mouth to tell him to stop, Alex snapped the man's neck.

The man fell down with a loud thud and died.

I heard screaming and I didn't know where it came from until I realised in that moment that I was the one screaming.

3

CHAPTER 3

I laid down on the bed, my wrists chained to the bed posts. The chains were made of iron and they hurt. I'm sure there will be bruises on my wrists once someone take the chains off me, that is if someone has the courage to do it.

That monster, whose name was Alex, as I heard is so cruel. He killed a member of the group in front of my eyes and I felt myself get torn apart. I knew I kept screaming for a long time and the next thing I know I am chained to a bed! The beast did it and then he left me like this as if it is not a big problem.

I huffed in anger and boredom. I have been sitting here for a good measure of time now and I would do anything to get out. Something inside me told me that I will never be able to escape from him and I know I'm right because he had made it crystal clear that I would never leave him.

An idea suddenly came to me and I felt stupid for not thinking about it earlier. I can't break chains made of iron of course but who said my wolf couldn't ?

I smirked as I shifted to my white wolf. The iron chain broke to pieces soaring through the air to different directions in the room. I felt free now.

I shifted to my human form and I dressed in one of his shirts and shorts. I hated the idea of being in his clothes but I can't leave naked.I also hated the idea that part of me was enjoying the feel of his clothes on me.

I went to the window and jumped through it for the second today. I landed with a loud thud and I prayed that nobody, mainly him, didn't hear me.

This was my second time I have tried to escape and I hoped I would be able to fully escape this time.

I was running in the forest, panting and looking behind me every minute to see if someone was behind me. I was terrified because if he found me, I am not sure what he will do but knowing him I'm sure he will make me suffer.

I arrived to a river and looked ahead to see that I was close to leaving his territory. I felt a rush of relief as I realised I was close to leaving this place, where until now I had gained nothing but learnt things I wished that I hadn't learnt, like the fact that he is my mate.

I began to move but stopped when I saw Alex ahead. He was talking to someone. I became anxious and nervous, I couldn't leave his territory now since he was ahead of me.

I took a deep breath and hid behind a tree. I decided that I will stay behind a tree until he leaves then I will be on my way. I prayed he wouldn't smell my scent.

I couldn't help but listen to their conversation but I didn't expect what heard.

"Alex, 3 rogues entered our territory right now," The man who was talking to Alex told him with a frown. "They were looking for a girl who we caught yesterday."

I gasped, they were talking about me. My group is looking for me and I couldn't help but feel that they should not try to look for me. Alex will kill them with no mercy.

"Have you caught them?" Alex asked angrily and I could tell he was fuming at the fact that rogues entered his territory.

"We caught one of them but the other two escaped," The man said in a low voice and Alex growled at him." The one we caught put up much of a fight. We tried to beat him but by that time the other two had escaped."

"I guess if he is that strong then he must be one of their leaders." Alex said with a smirk. I put my hand over my mouth to cover any sound I made, if it was one of our leaders then it would be a big problem since the leaders were the ones who kept us together and protected us.

"Yes I am aware of that, right now he is the room but he has done nothing but curse at us." The man told Alex.

"I am going to have some time with him and I don't want anyone to interrupt me." Alex told him in his Alpha voice and I could see an arrogant smirk making its way onto his face.

I am sure he will have fun torturing one of my leaders and that thought made me sick as the memory of him killing one of my members came back to me.

"I will go back now," The man informed Alex. "Is there any-thing you want?"

"I want you to check on the girl in my room and have some food sent to her. But I don't want you near her, don't touch her, don't talk to her, don't tell her anything and make sure that no one gets in her room. If you disobey me, I swear you won't live to see tomorrow." Alex threatened him and I had no doubt that he meant every word based on the way he spoke.

"I understand." The man as he nodded to him and went on his way.

I'm scared, Alex would now find out that I escaped and he will come after me but I can leave before he knows. I want to leave but can I leave one of my leaders to die ? That is not me.

But if I went there I would also be caught and the leader would be killed, no matter what I did. If I escaped then the leader would also be killed but I will be free. I realised in that situation that the leader will be killed but I can run away to inform my group of the circumstances then we can go rescue him.

I looked ahead to see Alex standing there and he seemed to be tense, as if holding himself from something. I wondered what happened that caused him to tense up. I watched him as he relaxed and made his way inside the forest, probably to his house where he would find me gone and I bet his expression would be priceless.

I waited till he was out of my sight then I ran ahead as fast as I could. I felt like I was near my freedom. I smiled brightly and I couldn't stop thinking about my group, I missed them.

I was running and thinking so deeply that I didn't realize someone was walking towards me until he stood in front of me blocking me path.

I looked up and gasped.

Alex

He was standing in front of me. His black eyes found my shocked ones. I stood stunned and frozen. His head titled to the side as if wondering how it is possible that I am standing there in front of him.

I didn't know what to do right now.

Run! My mind screamed to me and the next thing I know I'm running as I have never ran before. I looked behind me but he was no where to be seen. I gulped as he could be anywhere right now. I have never felt this terrified and I have never ran like this before.

While running at the side of the river, I heard a sudden growl that made me shiver. It came from my right side and I looked to see Alex sprinting towards me with a snarl on his face that I have never seen on him before.

He will catch me, I can feel it but I am not going to give up.

I turned to the left and I jumped into the river without a second thought. The water was cold but I forgot about it as I saw Alex dive into the water behind me. It was apparent he will not give up.

I swam quickly. I never knew I could swim this fast but I quickly stopped that thought as Alex began running towards me and I didn't know what he is planning to do but I knew it won't be pleasant at all.

I looked behind me only to regret it. He was 5 foot away from me and he will catch me any second.

I panicked and dove under the water. It wasn't the perfect solution but at least I will be away from him. I was wrong. An arm wrapped around my waist and I was tugged to the surface. We both grasped for breath as I spluttered out water.

I'm tired, my body ached almost everywhere. He watched me with his dark eyes.

I pushed him away and made my way to the side of the river but before I could push myself up Alex caught hold of my hips. He twisted me around to face him and his body pressed closer to mine.

"You ran away again." He said darkly though gritted teeth. It felt so much like a threat and I knew it was.

"Leave me alone, you monster!" I said angrily as I squirmed in his hold but he only held me tighter.

I wanted to cry. I'm tired, hungry and terrified of him. I didn't know what to do any longer.

He pulled me out of the river and climbed up the river bank. I'm drained of all energy. I knew I should fight him or anything but I couldn't. I'm so tired that I'm not able to do anything.

He pushed me on the ground and I tried to get up but he pushed my shoulders down roughly.

He climbed on me until he was on all fours above me.

He held my wrist above my head with one hand and the other hand he put on my waist, His evil slits rose to meet mine. He brought his mouth near my ear and whispered darkly.

"If you ever leave me again or even think about it, I will hunt you down and kill your family in front of you. " He threatened me.

Shivers ran through my body and fear took me whole.. I believed every word he said.

"Just leave me alone." I said in a low voice but he only looked at me darkly. Titling his head as if observing me.

"I would never leave you alone, you are mine and I would be damned if I ever let you go." He said in a serious voice.

"Fuck you!" I growled at him and tried to push him off me but his hold was so tight that I couldn't move.

He nuzzled my neck and he seemed to enjoy it. "You are only alive because you are my mate, sweetheart." He said in a soft voice. He is weird, one moment he was angry with me and the other he is being soft with me. He's bipolar.

"I will stay with you if you free the leader that you have." I said with despair and desperation in my voice.

He looked at me strangely then chuckled.

"I don't make deals and I for sure won't make a deal like this with you." He said with a smirk. He is beautiful, like a wolf painted in the moonlight and I did not know how someone as flawless as him was so cruel and ruthless.

"Then I won't stay with you ever." I growled at him and I really didn't know where that courage came from.

"You will stay by force if you remain this way." He told me while caressing my face and I almost leaned into his touch. The keyword here being almost.

"You can't do it, I won't tolerate it." I said in a tired voice.

"I can and I will," He glared at me. "If you escape one more time, I will hurt you and it will be painful." He said in a steady and low voice.

I didn't know what to do, I was lost and confused. I knew he meant every word he said in his warning and it scared me but he doesn't expect me to do everything he says, right?

He stood up and began to walk back to his house. He turned around to face me. "Come here," He demanded darkly.

I got up and walked to him slowly, I didn't want to go to him but if I didn't he will only get more angry and I didn't want to know what he will do then.

I walked to him slowly to annoy him but of course he would not have any of that.

He stormed towards me and in one swift movement, he had me over his shoulder. I hit him on his back but it was useless. Ignoring my protest, he started running back to his house.

I noticed he was running faster than anyone I had ever seen. I could only see the ground moving really fast. I was growing dizzy since I was upside down.

"Let me go!" I protested.

"Never," was his replay as he continued running while holding my legs tightly. "I am enjoying the view here." He told me in a seductive voice and I glared at his back.

When we arrived to the house, Alex put me down and grabbed my hand with more force than was necessary and dragged me to the house.

The man who was talking to Alex earlier came rushing to us and he was panting.

"Alex the rogue escaped, but we sent more men after and I am sure they will catch him." He told Alex in a hurry.

Alex growled so loudly that I was sure all were wolfs in the pack heard him. His eyes turned unbelievably darker and he let go of my hand and pushed me towards the man.

"Drew, stay with her and make sure she is safe inside the house! If anything happens to her or if anyone touches her, you will regret it." He growled at him.

Alex looked at me one final time then he shifted to his wolf and ran into the forest.

I turned to Drew who was smiling slightly at me but I was not focusing on him. My thoughts turned to the rogue who ran away. He is one of my leaders and by running away, I'm sure he wants to die.

I wished he didn't escape because I could have convinced Alex to be easy on him even if doubt that Alex would listen to me.

I made up my mind that if they caught him I would do everything in my power to not let Alex kill him. I mean anything because I knew deep down inside me that if Alex killed one more person in my group, I would not take it any more and I didn't know what I would do then.

4

— · —

CHAPTER 4

I have been sitting here, doing nothing at all except listening to Drew making a few comments on certain things, I tried to pay attention to what he was saying but I couldn't as my mind was on what Alex would do to the rogue. The memory of how he killed one of my group in front of my eyes came back to me and it brought unpleasant feeling.

I just wished that Alex wouldn't do that again because I won't be able to take it.

".... But really Alex is a nice person" Drew said looking at me.

"I am sorry but what were you saying?" I asked him with a small smile.

"You aren't paying attention to what I am saying, are you?" He asked with a smirk.

"No I am sorry, I just have a lot of things on my mind" I told him with a sigh and looked away.

"You are thinking about what Alex will do to the rogue when he catches him" Drew said simply with a shrug.

I was amazed that he could read my mind pretty easily.

"Do you think he can spare him this time, I mean he is one of my group " I told him, unable to continue because I really didn't know what to tell him.

Drew had a deep thought look on his face and he titled his head as if to observe me.

"No" He said casually.

"Why no ?" I asked and I crossed my arms over my chest to try to look serious.

"For the fact that Alex despise rogues and this rogue is one of the leaders so do you really think Alex will let him live ! " Drew told me as the answer was the most obvious thing in the world.

And in a way I guess it was because Deep inside me I knew that Alex will kill him and I was trying my best to ignore it.

I decided to ask a question who have been on my mind for a while.

"Why does Alex hate rogues so much ?" I asked but Drew gave me a look that said I was asking something stupid so I continued," I know all alphas hate rogues but it is clear that Alex hates them more than normal" I told him.

"That isn't for me to tell you, I guess Alex should tell you himself" Drew told me looking at the ground.

"I don't think he will ever tell me" I said with a heavy sight, "tell me and I will do anything you want" I said seriously because I wanted to know the answer.

"Well I do want something" He said seduatively, looking at me from head to toes slowly And I glared at him.

If looks could kill then he would be dead right now.

He just looked at me and laughed," You are really beautiful but I love my life and I seriously don't want Alex to kill me," He told in a low voice and I released he was serious, "I really wish you are my mate now" He said looking at me.

I blushed and I was about to answer when a group emitted from behind me.

Alex...

"Too bad she already has a mate who is your Alpha" He growled at Drew.

In a second, Drew stood up from the couch and he put on a blank face but I could tell he was afraid from the inside.

"don't worry, I won't tell him what you wanted before" I sent Drew the message through the mind link and I had to hold off my laugh as he shoot me a glare.

"I am here now, You can leave" Alex snapped at him. Drew looked quickly at me and began to walk away only to be stopped by Alex.

"I don't like you saying such things to my mate any more" Alex whispered darkly," You are my beta and I don't want to hurt you but if I saw you looking at her in a wrong way or talking like that again, I won't hesitate to cause you pain" He told him in a serious voice.

I shivered at the tone of his voice, Alex was so scary at time and I didn't prefer to be in his way at those times.

Drew nodded to him and left but not before he send me a message through the mind link.

"Remember when I told you Alex was nice guy ? scratch that ! "

This time I couldn't hold back the laugh and I laughed for the first time since I got here.

I could now say that I made a friend, The beta of my mate.

"What is so funny?" Alex said in bewilderment after Drew had left.

"Nothing, I just remembered something!" I told him.

"I will let this drop but for now only" He said in a low voice and walked towards me.

He looked down at me and held my face between his hand and began nuzzling my neck.

"I missed you" He whispered in my ear and tingles shoot through my body.

I almost wanted to let him hold me like this for the rest of my life but the keyword here is ..... Almost.

"Did you catch him ?" I asked him, looking into his eyes.

Please say no ...

"Yes of course." He said simply," He was a fool for running away in the first place but I already gave him what he deserves" He said with a glint in his eyes.

I flinched at the idea that he enjoyed doing this but I already know that but still it didn't help to make me feel any better.

" What did you do to him?" I asked carefully.

"It is None of your business" He growled at me and sat on the coach.

"It is since I am now the Luna of the pack then I have to know everything that happens in the pack" I said with a triumph smile.

"You are right" He told me casually and I smirked, I already know I was but then he continued, " You will know everything thing about the pack but not about the rogues considering you were one of them" He said.

I couldn't believe him, He seriously couldn't think that I will let him hurt any more members of my group.

"If you do anything to that rogue, I swear I will hate you forever" I said looking at him in the eyes.

He looked at me and chuckled, " You can't do that, You are my mate and you already know that"

He was right, I knew that. I certainly couldn't ignore the feeling I have for him now and as much as I am trying to ignore them, I can't.

"Maybe you are right but I will never let you touch me" I told him and I was honest about that.

In three longs strides, He was in front of me. He placed his hands on my hips and growled.

"You are my mate, Mine" He growled at me and his claws extended and they cut through my clothes.

"I know but It is possible to reject a mate" I said as I wrapped my arms around his neck.

He was beyond furious, His eyes turned to a dark shade and he was shaking with anger.

"You are my mate, I can have you when I please" He snapped at me and tightened his hold on me.

"Then the only way to do it is to force me" I told him seriously and I knew that even if he was coldhearted, He will never force me.

He took deep calming breaths and then began nuzzling my mark on my neck.

"What is your name?" He asked and I was surprised, I didn't think he will ask me this right now.

"I will tell you when you promise me not to hurt him" I said and of course my words made him angry.

"I won't make any deal with you, I will be his worst nightmare" He told me with an arrogant smirk.

"Fine but you will never know my name" I told him as with all my strength, I pulled away from him and walked away.

He was fuming, He looked at me one last time before he stormed out of the house.

There was two possibilities now, He will punish the rogue more cruelly because of what I had said or not hurt him to know my name. I hoped it was the the last one.

Knowing him, He would probably choose the first one and would be careless about what I say but it isn't wrong to wish that he will listen to me this one time and won't do anything to hurt him because of me.

5

CHAPTER 5

Kicking the sheets from my body, I didn't release I went to go to sleep, the last thing I remember is that Alex left and I kept on wondering around the house. I wasn't entirely sure how I got in bed actually.

My hard pillow that I was laying under seemed to be the cause of all that heat.

Sighing lazily, I tired to roll away but a hot fabric was wrapped around my waist tightly, preventing me from moving.

I tried to untangle myself but couldn't, something was keeping me in my place. I squirmed for a while but then went limp with a huff.

"I Now know how to control myself near you" A seduative voice whispered hotly in my ear.

I screamed and tried to push him away but he was keeping me in his hold, His hold only tightened and he chuckled.

I know that voice ...

I turned around and came face with face to Alex, He was smirking down at me. I blushed at his closeless.

He ran his hand up my back until my forehead where he pushed my brown hair away from my face.

I sat up, escaping his hold and he was caught off guard. He tried to embrace me but I moved away from his grasp. He frowned in frustration.

"You are so hot" I frowned at him, remembering how I woke feeling so hot, I felt like my skin was about to melt off.

"I already know that" He said with that arrogant smirk of his as he ran his hand through his midnight black hair.

"I didn't mean it that way" I told him and I could feel myself blushing.

Unfortunately, He wasn't paying attention as his eyes moved down and stared at the huge opening in my shirt i was wearing that gave a generous view of My bra covered boobs.

I tried to calm myself in order not to lash at him.

"Pervent" I hissed in a low voice crossing my arms over my chest.

He looked at me as if nothing happened, "Don't blame me, Your body is a killer and you have the face of an angel," He said in a low voice and I tried not to be much fluttered by his words.

"Whatever" I told him in a huff.

I got off the bad and then I remembered that I didn't take a shower for 2 days and I wanted to take one now but I didn't feel safe with Alex and his hormones around me. I know he wanted to mate with me but I was in no way ready for that and I was sure he was aware of it.

"I want to take a shower and I need proper clothes now" I demanded, Alex eyes narrowed and his mouth twitched. He didn't say anything, He just got off the bed and in one long stride, He was standing in front of me.

I looked up and up and up ..... Hell he was so tall ! I reached below his shoulders. He was so hot and A rush of lust shot down my spine sending goosebumps all over my skin.

"Fine, the bathroom is over there" He told me as he pointed towards a door behind me.

I looked behind me and indeed there was a door, I nodded at him and made my ways towards the bathroom. I reached to open the door but I felt there was someone towering over me from behind.

I looked around me slowly to find Alex right behind me, I frowned in confusion, "Why are you following me?" I demanded sternly.

"I can't leave you alone there" He shrugged as it was nothing important.

He reached behind me and opened the door then he brought his mouth near my ear, "After you princess" He whispered hotly in my ear and I shivered. I almost gave in to him and was about to enter with him but I shook my head.

I pushed him away but he hardly moved as He was so much stronger than me. He narrowed his eyes and titled his head as to observe me.

"You aren't coming with me!" I said in a low voice, He was about to argue but I continued, "And that is final" I told him sternly.

He kept staring at me and I saw the moments when he unwillingly nodded to me.

"Make it quick" He whispered then went away and sat on the bed, staring at me.

As much as I hated to admit it, I already felt drawn to Alex and as much as I tried to fought it, I couldn't. There was that strong bond between us that I couldn't shake off but I know it was because he is my mate but still I didn't like the idea of being drawn to him so quickly when he had made me so angry so many times.

I sighed as I looked around the bathroom, it was so modern and I loved it. Alex was so rich, That was obvious. All Alphas and Betas were rich.

I turned on the shower and got in after detaching my clothes on the floor. The hot water ran along my body and I had some time to thing about all what happened since the moment I entered the pack.

I finished my shower and fortunately, I found that Alex left me one of his shirts and one of his shorts. I preferred to have my clothes but I didn't have much of a choice right now.

I got out of the bathroom and found the room empty, weird, As far as I know Alex, He wouldn't just leave me here alone.

Out of nowhere, I bumped into a wall. I looked up and released that it wasn't a wall but Alex towering over me with his usual smirk.

"Finally finished, If you took any longer I would have come in and got you myself" He hummed in a low sexy voice.

I noticed he was shirtless now And his gorgeous chest. He now loomed over me, sexually threatening me.

"I am glad I finished then" I said with a huff as I crossed my arms over my chest, trying to look serious.

He crossed his massive arms over his thick chest and I almost drooled at the sights of flesh.

Was it that wrong to have naughty images flash through her mind about the her mate who with no doubt had planned to keep her with him forever against her will.

He was hot, strong and straight up manly.

"I am going to take a shower, Stay right here and don't go anywhere" He said in a firm voice and was about to leave.

"Wait, The rogue,what did you do to him?" I said biting my lower lip, I forget about him and I didn't know how but I guess it was because of everything that is going on right now.

He clenched his fists and he appeared to be trying to calm himself down. He finally looked at me, "He is alive but in the pack prison and He isn't getting out anytime soon" He told me and looked away.

"You let him live" I said as I released a breath,"I thought you were going to kill him,Why? I asked him in a whisper but I am sure he heard me.

He seemed unwilling to answer me but he stormed towards me and held my face between his hands. He caressed my face softly and I leaned into his touch.

"I didn't kill him because of you" He told me softly and in that moment my feeling only increased for him. The thought that Alex who killed any rogue he found, Didn't kill one because of me made me feel closer to him.

He looked at me one final time before he entered the bathroom and closed the door. I know he must feel weak because he didn't kill him but I hoped he wasn't.

I moved and sat on the bed and looked around and then is when I noticed it ....

A cell phone

I hurried to it and quickly dialed my mother's number, She must be so worried about me right now and I didn't like to be the cause of it.

I waited for a few seconds but she didn't pick up and I was worried that something happened to her. I dialed the next person who came to my mind after it.

Will, He was my best friend since I was a child and he was like a brother to me. I know that now he would be worried sick about me. He was so protective around me and I couldn't take it sometimes but I know he did it because he cared for me greatly and didn't want anything to happen to me.

"Hello" Will answered the phone and I didn't release how much I missed him till now.

"Will" I said with a smile, I couldn't describe my happiness at finally hearing one of my group's voice.

"Elizabeth, Where the fuck are you ! I am worried sick about you and I have been searching for you non stop" He shouted at him and I understood his anger.

"I am fine, How are you and how is my mother, is she okay ? Why isn't she answering?" I asked him and I couldn't keep the worry from my voice.

"We are okay Beth but where are you ? Tell me where you are and I will come and get you right now!" He snapped at me. I winced, I didn't like him being angry at me but I understood his reason.

"Will I found my mate and he is kinda keeping me here for a while" I said slowly and he was about to argue but I interrupted him, "I cant tell you where I am because I know you will come and I don't know if he will stop himself from... hurting you" I chose the right word after some time. I couldn't tell Will that my mate is going to kill you just because you are a rogue but I knew Alex wouldn't take it well if he knew that Will is coming to get me.

"Beth what is the fuck ! Just tell me where you are now" He told me in a stern voice.

"Bye Will, I will miss you but I am fine so don't worry about me" I said in a soft voice, He was like a brother from another mother and I didn't want to make him worry about me.

"I love you so much" I told him And I was about to hung up when a demonic growl seemed to vibrate all around me. I gasped and backed up slowly, I could hear Will shouting at me though the phone about what was going on but I couldn't concentrate.

In the doorway, stood Alex with strained muscles, He flexed his hands in a threatening manner. His teeth were bared and the veins bulged from his bare arms and chest.

I decided to remain quite and keep it safe.

The anger that swarmed around him thickly wasn't all aimed at me. He was fuming and I saw him eyeing the phone in my hand then he snapped his eyes back to me looking at me angrily.

He snarled at me and that is when It hit me, He misunderstood the phone call and I was about to explain to him but I saw him storming towards me with clenched fists.

He had that predator look on his face that was aimed at the prey and to my horror I was that prey.

6

CHAPTER 6

I was truly scared as Alex came towards me with cold and angry eyes, his jaw was clenched and he looked like he wanted to break something.He immediately appeared in front of me, taking the cell phone away from my hands and smashing it to the floor.Shaking with fear at whatever he was about to do, I stood up and moved to the wall on the opposite side.

He stormed towards me and pushed me to wall, locking both of my hands with one of his. Saying he was angry was an understatement, He was clearly furious."It was just..." I cleared my throat, feeling like I couldn't speak then I gained my strength and glared at him, "That was absolutely rude from you""I never said I wasn't rude" He snarled at me and I remembered I watched something about predator and the prey, Never move or do anything to provoke the predator so I decided to follow that now because I didn't want to make Alex angrier than he was."Who was he? I heard his voice and from the way you are speaking you two seem very close" He snapped at me as leaned to me, He held my chin to make me look in his eyes."A friend" I sluttered out looking at him, he titled his head to the side not quite believing me."I don't believe you!" He said angrily as he shook his head, "Tell me who he is Now before I hunt him down and kill him slowly and painfully myself, Elizabeth".Shit ! He can't be serious but looking in his eyes, I knew he was serious.

He had that mean and ruthless look in his eyes and I didn't know how he knew my name but I remembered that he must have heard Will through the phone."Suit yourself then ! He is only my friend and I don't know what I can do to make you believe me" I said getting angry now because he didn't trust me.He pulled away from me and grabbed the Cell phone from the floor and to my shock, it still works.He gave it to me and stared angrily at me, "Call him" He mused as he waited impatiently for me "Loud speaker" He smirked at me.Of course he was going to ask that, I wanted to tell him no but at the same time, I wanted him to see that he can trust me.I dialed Will's number and he answered after the first ring."Elizabeth Are you okay ? Who was the person ? is he hurting you ? tell me where you are so I can and teach that man a lesson for hurting you ! I swear if he touched you I will kill him" He shouted angrily and I rolled my eyes at him. He was over protective sometimes.Alex laughed then he took the phone from my hands before I could even blink."Listen pup, I don't want you to talk to Elizabeth again, She is mine and mine only ! if I see you talking to her ever again, I promise you that you will regret it" Alex shouted at him then tossed the phone on the bed.

I was fuming Alex had no right to just shout at Will like this when he didn't do anything wrong, Now I was scared that Will would come here and I know Alex wouldn't hesitate to kill him as he was a rogue.Alex turned to me and wrapped his arms around my waist, bringing me closer to him and nuzzling my neck."Are you crazy?" I shouted to him, trying with all of my strength to push him but he didn't even move from his place, "He was like a brother to me, You can't just go and threaten him like that" I told him as I struggled to release myself from his hold."But he isn't related to you by blood so a possibility is still very real" He barked right back as he tightened his hold on me, " I don't like you talking to him anymore" He growled at me.Then he took my lips in a mind shattering kiss, Heat shot through me. His lips were firm, smooth and masculine. His large hands travelled down my arms, over my stomach, past my hips, pausing at my thighs. He hoisted my legs up and open forcing me to wrap them around his waist. I moaned at the amazing sensation. I tried to kiss him back to the best of my abilities but ended up baring my teeth against his.

He chuckled as he removed his lip from me, to my disappointment. He placed me back on the floor and moved his hand through my hair softly.That was the best kiss I ever had, He made me feel so beautiful and desired.I remembered our argument before and became angry because I let my guard slip down around him when I was supposed to be angry at him.I pushed him away and he looked surprised, "Get out so I can get dressed" I told him as I crossed my arms over my chest.He frowned at my behavior but he nodded unwillingly and left without a second word. He looked angry because I pushed him away but he deserve it because of the way he spoke to Will.After dressing I left the room and went downstairs, I expected to find Alex downstairs but I didn't find him anywhere.I looked around nervously because I was sure Alex would never leave me alone."Good morning, Beautiful " A voice whispered in my ear and the next thing I know, two arms wrapped around my waist hoisting me up from the floor.I kicked at whoever was holding me and forced my arm backwards to the person's chest and his hold weakned as I stood up and prepared to hit the person in the face.I was shocked to see Drew standing there, holding his stomach and moaning in pain.I giggled at the way he looked, I didn't regret hitting him He was the one who scared me."wow, that is tough" He told me as he finally stood up and chuckled, " feisty, I like that" He said as sat on the coach.I rolled my eyes at him and decided that this was typical him and he wouldn't stop teasing me."Aren't you afraid that Alex might hear you" I told him back smirking at him."He left ten minutes ago and told me not to talk to you, not to touch you and don't flirt with you" He mused as he chuckled."And you already done all that in five minutes" I told him and I saw him shrug.

I knew if Alex was here, Drew wouldn't dare to do all these things.I liked Drew's company a lot, He was my only friend here and I didn't want Alex to hurt him seeing that Drew was always flirting with me but I knew that Drew was a ladies man so I decided to ignore it."What do you think about going to the mall now?" I said excitedly. I wanted to get out of this house, I was really bored."And have Alex kill me for taking you out?" He looked at me like I was stupid and shook his head," No thanks"I thought to myself then an evil idea came to me. I smirked at Drew who looked at me like I was really crazy."I would never forgive You if Alex hurt me in anyway!" Drew told me in a low serious voice as he drove to the mall. I chuckled at his expression, You might be wondering what I did to make him come with me ?Well, I threatened Drew to tell Alex that he tried to kiss me. Of course Drew didn't even do that but it was the only idea that came to me to make Drew take me to the mall."Don't worry, if Alex saw us I will tell him I forced you here" I told him as I laughed at him, His expression was priceless. I could say he was furious with me right now.

After walking through the mall for three hours and buying more clothes than I would need, We left the mall and Drew was hoping that Alex didn't return home now. Drew paid for all the things I bought, I refused at first but he insisted.Drew drove so fast back to the house and I didn't appreciate it, He was trying to get me home before Alex.A white sport car appeared behind us and a smile tugged on my lips which Drew notice."How can you be smiling at a time like this, I have to get us home before Alex arrives and find you missing" He said as he shook his head."Alex is behind us now" I told him, pointing to the reviewer mirror.Drew looked at the mirror and gasped."Shit ! This is all you fault, Elizabeth. He looks furious now" He said."Keep your eyes on the road and pull over at the next stop, I will get down and calm him and you go away, He will make you pull over if you didn't stop" I told him as I pointed to the side of the road.He nodded and stopped the car and I quickly got down but not before hearing a good luck from Drew.

Alex stopped the car suddenly and got out, He reached me in no time with his long strides."Are you okay?" He asked as he held my face.I nodded to him."Get in the car" His voice had finality in it and I knew that this wasn't time to argue with him.We drove in silence, Alex was fuming as he was gripping the sterring wheel so hard."I will make Drew regret taking you while I wasn't with you" He growled at me."Alex I was the one who told him to take me" I said calmly, I didn't want Alex hurting Drew, I know I wont be able to take it."But he went against my orders and took you outside" He said in a low voice.I tried to argue back but he interrupted, "Don't worry, I will get to you after him, You know I don't like You out of the house without me because I want to keep you safe all the time but you still went out with him" He told me.I won't give up, I would take all the blame but I would never let Alex do anything to drew, I swore it.We arrived to the house and Alex quickly got out and went inside. I followed after him because I still need to talk to him.He entered a guest room and I was about to enter but he closed the door."Alex, please hear me out ! I wanted to get out because I was bored and I made Drew take me, I will take the whole blame" I said as I banged on the door.

I felt tears streaming down my cheeks, I felt like I betrayed Alex which in a way I did. I sat in the floor, resting my hand against the door and before I knew it I was asleep.I woke up to find myself in a bed, I raised my eyebrows in confusion at the way I got here but looking at my left, I saw Alex sleeping and snoring lightly. I smiled knowing that he carried me here. I caressed his face softly as he slept. He looked so peaceful.He leaned into my touch and murmured, "Emma, Don't leave and go with him"I pulled my hand away quickly and felt a pang in my chest. Who was she ? was she is ex girlfriend ? I know she must mean a lot to him if he is murmuring about her in his sleep.I knew the next words that came out from his mouth will leave my world spinning out of control and my heart nearly stopping. I didn't release that these words would hurt this much."Emma, Don't go with him. You mean so much to me" He murmured softly.

7

CHAPTER 7

I sat, glaring at the wall behind Alex. We were having break-fast and now more than ever I wanted him out of the house so he could leave me in peace.

I didn't get how he could be so possessive of me and jealous when I talk to other men and he is the one who keep secrets about another woman from me but thinking about it again, Maybe he knew more than just one woman.

"Elizabeth, You hardly touched your food. What is wrong, baby?" He asked me, the concern was apparent in his voice but I chose to ignore it.

"None of your business" I snapped at him and he frowned deeply at me then smirked arrogantly at me.

"That is because of Drew, isn't it?" He mused as he focused his attention on me.

I signed as I remembered the fight we had in the morning....
Flash back

"Drew isn't coming today" Alex told me as he got ready for the day.

I was too busy thinking who was that Emma and I thought of asking him but I didn't really expect him to admit it.

"Is he okay?" I asked, now really worried about Drew. Thoughts of what Alex may have done to him came in my mind.

"Yes but he isn't come to look out for you from today" He growled at me and I gasped.

"He didn't do anything ! I am the one to blame so don't do this" I said to him with despair in my voice.

Alex chucked at me, "I am doing this to punish you, seeing how you enjoy his company and now you aren't going to see him any time soon" He smirked at me.

End of flashback

I never felt so much anger in my life, we had a long argument about it but in the end, Alex ignored me and went downstairs to have breakfast.

"If Drew isn't here by tomorrow, I would never let you touch me" I told him and I remembered using that threat with him before and it worked so it may work again.

"I am going to have you sooner or later, We both know it" He told me as he got up and came towards me.

He held my hands and caressed them softly , "I don't want to fight with you anymore, I hate it. You mean so much to me that I can't take it" He told as he caressed my face but I quickly pushed his hand away.

He said these exact words but to some other woman than me, I felt disgusted with him right now.

"Is it me who mean so much to you or a woman called Emma" I snapped at him as I crossed my arms over my chest.

I finally let the words out, I couldn't keep them to myself anymore.

He seemed shocked for a second then composed himself, He titled his head to the side as to observe me.

"Who is Emma?" He asked and he appeared confused but I won't buy it.

"You said her name while you were sleeping yesterday" I growled as I again felt the pang in my chest. It really hurt and as mush as I wanted to know the truth about Emma, I was afraid that the truth will crash me and I knew that I won't be able to take it.

"I don't know anyone by the name of Emma" He told me softly as he held my face between his hands.

"You said her name so she must mean something to you" I told him in agony, He looked to be saying the truth but I want to make sure.

"There is no Emma in my life" He told me as he ran his hand through my hair, "I expect honesty from you and for that I will always be honest with you" He told me as he pulled my in a tight hug.

"You are the only one for me, Beth" He whispered softly in my hair and I forgot all about Emma, He looked honest about what he said.

I was still not so entirely sure about what he said but now I felt myself melting into his embrace, too much happened to my life till now and I didn't have it in myself to keep arguing now.

It was almost 4 hours since Alex left and All that time, I have been sitting alone. Alex assigned five werewolfs out of the house to guard me and it annoyed me that who could think of me as so weak but again he was really overprotective.

I was laying on my bed, thinking about what happened to me so far. Too many things happened that I never expect to happen now, One of them was finding Alex.

Suddenly there was a knocking on the window, I quickly stood up and looked towards the window.

I gasped as I couldn't contain my shock

There knocking on the window was Will, how did he get here? How could he have been not noticed or the fact that Alex will come back at any time.

I reached the window in 2 long strides and opened it quickly.

"I thought you weren't going to open any time soon" He said with a smile as he got in and closed the window behind him.

"Will you-" I didn't have time to talk as he grabbed my hand and dragged me to the window.

"We have to leave before Your mate comes back" He said in a hurry as he dragged but I forced my feel to the ground to stop him.

"I can't come with you" I whispered as I looked to see his confused gase.

"Why?" He looked at me as I was crazy to say that.

"If Alex comes and find me gone, He will kill all our group," I said honestly as I looked in his eyes, "Starting with you" I told him the last part seriously because it is what it is going to happen.

"We could escape somewhere where he can't find us, you can't stay with him, He is so cruel. How can you take it!" He said angrily at me and I understood that he was concerned for my safely.

"I honestly don't know but I know I have to stay here with him, He is my mate" I told him with a small smile as I looked down.

"Elizabeth are you-" He was interrupted but the door opening, I was horrified thinking that it was Alex but thankfully it was Drew.

I opened my mouth to speak to him but the next thing I know is that Drew had his hand around Will's throat against the wall, He was choking him, to my horror.

I ran to Drew and began to push him but he wouldn't budge.

"Drew let him go, He is my friend!" I shouted at him.

He looked at me for a second then at Will and he unwillingly let him go, Will fell to the ground gasping for breath.

I rushed to him and made sure he was okay but then Will looked at me angrily.

"You want to stay here," He growled at me, "With those monsters ".

I cringed at the last words but I couldn't blame him, In a way they were really monsters.

Drew came towards me and stood next to me, Glaring at Will. Drew was a beta so that meant he was way stronger than Will and he could beat him in less than 10 seconds.

"If you don't leave in 10 minutes you pup, I will tell the Alpha and he will personally deal with you" Drew growled at Will and these words coming from his mouse, sounded that it was normal for him to threaten anyone this way.

I thought Drew was different but to my sadness, He wasn't. He was just like them but a little better or so I thought.

"I am already leaving, I came here for no reason it seems" He growled at me and I stepped back.

Will has never been so angry with me before and I felt a pang in my chest at the thought he was that angry with me.

"Will, I am so sorry" I told as I felt the tears gathering in my eyes, I couldn't really help it. Will was like my brother and I couldn't stand the thought of him angry at me.

Will chuckled darly as he looked at me, "I don't know any-more Elizabeth, I hope you have a nice life here which I highly doubt" He told me and the next thing, He jumped out of the window and shifted.

I couldn't hold back the tears any longer, I wasn't the person to cry because I didn't like to make people see this way but I couldn't stop as I started to cry and I could feel my wolf howling at pain.

Drew wrapped his arms around me and whispered calming words to me but I pushed him away. I didn't want to be around him or anyone now.

"Leave me alone" I snapped at him as I pushed him away from me. He looked at me for a second before opening the door.

"If you tell Alex anything, I would never forgive you" I said in a low voice but I knew he heard me.

His body tensed but then he relaxed and he was out of the room.

I wasn't worried because deep down I knew that Drew won't tell Alex as he valued my friendship or so I kept telling myself.

It was 2 house until I finally calmed down and went down-stars. I didn't want to talk to anyone yet as I was too angry and still hurt about Will. The thought of him make me tear up a little.

I saw Drew sitting on the coach, reading something but I had no idea what but I didn't care.

I acted as if he was never here and went to the kitchen, All the way there, I could feel his eyes on me.

"Aren't you going to ask how Alex allowed me here? Drew said with a smirk as he came towards me.

"I don't care" I shrugged, I didn't want to hear about Alex or anyone from his pack right now.

"He told me that you were sad that I won't come anymore but the next thing I knew, Alex told me to come here to cheer you up" He told me smiling at me.

I chose to ignore him, I didn't care about anything now.

Drew looked down at me and put his hand under my chin and raised my face to look at him.

"Don't be like this, I hate how you are now" He whispered as he looked at me with pity in his eyes.

I pushed his hand away and glared at him.

"You will have to deal with it" I said angrily and was about to say more but there was a knock on the door.

I moved before Drew and walked to the door quickly, thinking that I want to go out and leave the house now.

I opened the door and saw a beautiful woman standing infront me. She was around my age. She had blue eyes and her hair was blond and long. I felt like I couldn't compare to her.

She looked me up and down and frowned, "Who are you?" She asked me as she looked at me disapprovingly. I didn't know what she didn't like about me but I didn't like her already.

"I should be the one asking who you are considering this is my house" I said with a smirk as I saw her staring at me confused.

She smiled at me and smirked arrogantly at me as she ran her hand though her hair.

"I am Emma"

I gasped as I truly didn't believe her. I thought that she didn't exist since Alex told me so but looking at her now, standing infront of me, made me fuming with anger at Alex.

I was the stupid one to believe when he was lying to me so easily, if anyone was to blame then it would be me for believing him.

I wanted to close the door in her face but something behind her gained my attention.

A huge black wolf was growling so loudly and running towards us but he got closer.

I realized that it was Alex's wolf and I could see he was furious. I wondered what could have made him so angry to make him shift into his wolf form.

The answer to my question came to me sooner than I expect as I saw his wolf standing infront of Emma and growling so loudy and baring his teeth to here as he looked ready to...

Attack her !

I didn't know what to do, stop Alex or let him attack her since I already disliked her but I knew that I will take the first choice but Emma's next words stopped me.

"Alex, you think that will scare me" She said as she chuckled.

Now more than ever, I wanted to know who she was because Alex looked ready to kill her and she wasn't scared at all, instead she was laughing.

I know two things for sure that Alex had explaining to do and that this day wasn't one of my best days.

8

CHAPTER 8

Time seemed to slow by as Alex made his way towards Emma who by now still didn't move from her place, I wondered how she wasn't afraid from Alex when he looked that furious. I only saw him like this once when I escaped from him and I never wanted to be in his way again when he was angry because he looked really scary.

Alex's wolf stood in front of Emma and growled at her, sending shivers through me.

I knew I had to do something, I couldn't just let him hurt her.

I quickly moved in front of her, blocking Alex from going any further towards her.

He growled at me but I didn't move Although the way he looked right now scared me.

He shifted back to his human form and stood there fully naked in front of us. I blushed as i looked at him. His body was so tempting and I stopped myself from looking any lower.

I didn't notice when he stormed towards me and grabbed my wrist in an iron grip. It hurt but before I could complain any more. He pushed me towards Drew.

"Get her inside." Alex snarled keeping his eyes on me, probably mad because I stood in his way.

Drew nodded and pulled me behind him but I squirmed in his hold and I was able to get my arms from his grasp.

"What are you doing?" I asked as I placed my hands on Alex's chest, trying to calm him down.

"I am going to show her what happens when she messes with me." He said lowly, staring at her. His eyes were turning black and I knew his wolf was coming out again.

"I won't go inside" I said sternly to him.

My words made him mad, that was obvious.

"I said go inside and I don't want to repeat it again or you will be punished" He said it slowly and I know he meant every word by the look in his eyes.

I was about to protest again but Drew grabbed my hand and pulled, with more force this time, to the house.

I almost forgot about Emma who was standing there with an amused grin on her face. I didn't know what was wrong with her since I never saw anyone from the pack who doesn't fear Alex as her.

Drew cleared his throat and smiled at me, I thought he was crazy because I didn't know why he was smiling at a situation like this.

"Why are you smiling?" I said as I raised my eyebrows at him.

"You clearly don't know her, right?" He said with an amused look as he chuckled.

"Nope, How can I?" I said sarcastically, rolling my eyes at him.

"I thought that Alex would tell you" He shrugged as it was nothing important, "seeing that you are his mate"

His words made me angry because what he said was true but the truth was that Alex hid things from me and he never told me even though I am his mate.

"Never mind" I said, as I moved towards him and sat beside him on the coach.

If I was getting any answers then I know it would be right now from Drew.

"Drew, who is she?" I told him in a serious voice to make him pay attention to me.

Drew looked at me for a moment then signed as he put his hand under my chin and raised my eyes to look at him.

"Emma is his sister but Alex forced her out of the pack 3 years ago." He said as he let me go and waited to see my reaction.

I suddenly felt as if a heavy weight was lifted from my shoulders, Emma was his sister, Not his lover or girlfriend. I never felt so happy about something before. My jealousy was slowly killing me to know that Alex had feelings for another woman than me. But now knowing that Emma was just his sister was like a burden lifted from my shoulders.

"Why did Alex do that?" I asked him, ignoring the confused look he gave me at my happy state.

"I-" He was about to continue when the front door was opened suddenly and came A fuming alex. I was so used to him being angry by now.

"Out." He muttered as he looked at Drew, I cast drew a look, begging him not to leave me alone with Alex now.

He cast me an apologetic look but I saw the smirk on his face before he left.

I looked at Alex now and his jaw was clenched and he was taking deep breaths as to control his anger. He was dressed in black shorts right now and I was thankful for that.

I turned around and began to walk away, to anywhere away from him because it was best to leave him alone now.

"I didn't tell you to walk away." He snarled at me and I looked at him and he was clearly mad.

"I don't need your permission." I said slowly and I didn't know where that courage came from.

"don't walk away from me" He shouted in his alpha voice. I smirked and crossed my arms over my chest.

"Or what?" challenging him.

He kept his eyes fixed on me and smirked at me.

I made my way towards the stairs to see what he will do but I didn't even take two steps when suddenly He placed me over his shoulder, with one swift movement. I had a clear view of his back. He placed his hand below my thighs.

"Put me down." I shouted as I began to hit his back but he simply ignored me.

He reached our room and dumped me on the bed. I glared at him as I landed hard.

He was staring at me and his stare was so intense, I had no idea what to do but he broke the silence.

"You defied my orders, again" He said in a low voice but his eyes gave away how angry he was.

I looked at him and was about to speak but he cut me off.

"You underminded me in front of a pack member" He said in a cold voice and I know he was referring to drew.

"I didn't do anything." I said because I really didn't feel like I did anything wrong.

"You aren't allowed to do that anymore" He growled and stalked towards me.

"So basically I have to follow you every order and not have an opinion in anything!" I said sarcastically.

"You are beginning to catch up." He smirked at me as he climbed on the bed above me. I tried to push him away but it was pointless as he took both of my wrists and pinned them with one of his hands.

"You are unbelievable" I huffed as I struggled to get him off me, his hot breath was against my neck, making me unable to think clearly.

"Am I?" He told me as he nuzzled my neck.

I was about to speak when he crashed his lips on me, I tried to pull away but finally gave up. It sent waves of pleasure through me and I forgot about what happened.

He trailed kisses along my jaw and neck, rubbing himself on me in the process. He was holding tightly on my waist and sucking on the mark of my claim and I couldn't stop the moan that escaped my mouth.

He brought his mouth towards my ears.

"I want you" He said in a husky voice.

I couldn't contain the excitement that built up inside me. Should I stop him? Was I ready? Too many questions ran through my head but at the moment, I forgot everything. I only wanted him.

He grabbed the hem of dress and slowly started rising it up and over my body. He scanned my body lustfully and I couldn't stop the blush that appeared on my cheeks.

"You are so beautiful" He whispered hotly in my ear.

I felt naked in only my bra and panties. He slowly brought his hands from my thights, to my waist.

The tone of the phone ringing made him froze. I heard a growl emit from Alex and he unwillingly reached out to grab his phone.

"What?" He growled out, sounding furious but then his eyes got wide and I saw his eyes full of worry. I immediately know that there was something dangerous that took place.

He ended the call and with a quick glance at me, went to the door. I was hurt that he payed me no more than a glance.

"Alex" I called out to him.

"I have to go" He said quickly then he locked eyes with me, "just be glad the phone interrupted, I wouldn't have been able to stop myself" He said in a low voice as his eyes darken with last then he quickly got of the room, leaving me with my thoughts.

Bang

I quickly got out of the bed and dressed, I knew that there is something downstairs then I heard voice. People shouting and Alex's growling.

I ran downstairs and nearly screamed at the scene in front of me.

Emma, lying on the floor and she was wounded and her clothes had spots of blood on them and she was unconscious. Alex was holding her in his arms and barking orders to the people behind him to grab a doctor.

I was frozen at my place, I could see the scared look on Alex's face, I know He and Emma didn't apparently get along but she was his sister after all.

I moved towards them to help in any way possible but Alex's growl made me stop.

"Get to the room and don't ever get down unless I told you" He snapped at me as held Emma.

"I-" I began to speak but he interrupted me.

"Get up please, I can't stand the thought of you getting hurt" He said more softly and I never saw Alex look this vulnerable before till this moment.

I nodded and got up but stopped when Drew came in, gasping for breath.

"Alex they are here" He said quickly.

Alex's eyes turned to midnight black and he stood up, after placing Emma gently on the ground.

"Bring the our fighters, those bastards will wish they were never born" His voice was full of malice. It made me shiver from its tone.

"Already done Alpha" He nodded.

"Take care of them" He told me and I knew he was referring to emma and me but right now I wanted to go with him, to make sure he was safe. I felt pain at the though of him getting hurt.

But I didn't have my time as Alex shifted and went sprinting outside the house. I ran after him and was about to shift if it weren't for Drew's iron grip around my waist.

"Stay, he is going to be okay" He whispered to reassure me but I didn't care. I wanted to go to Alex to help him but I couldn't as much I squirmed to get out of Drew's Arms.

"Who are they?" I said angrily as Drew just couldn't leave me alone.

"They are rogues" He said slowly but I didn't expect the next words that came from his mouth.

"They are from the group who killed his parents."

9

CHAPTER 9

2 hours since Alex left and I was worried sick about him, I couldn't think of anything else except him and how he is doing. Alex was one of the strongest Alphas ever even this thought didn't calm me.

Gazing at Emma who had been unconscious since the attack, I felt sorry for her and I hoped she would be okay soon. I still didn't know what she did to deserve such harsh punishment from Alex but I intended to know and probably help them to make up in the process.

"She is going to be okay." A voice muttered from behind me and I turned around to see Drew, Standing there and I didn't miss the worried look in his eyes.

"She was your friend?" I asked him.

Drew shrugged and went to sit on the chair opposite to me which was next to Emma's bed.

"Well yea, She never liked me though." Drew trailed off as if remembering something.

"Why?"

"Because she always thought I was bad influence on Alex," He said slowly, "Little did she know that Alex was bad influence on me." He chuckled as he said this.

I couldn't help but giggle, I knew he was trying to lighten the mood and it was working but whatever he did, he couldn't erase my worry on Alex.

"There seems to be problems between her and Alex." I told him and I saw him stiffen.

"You should be asking Alex, not me." He said as he got up and made his way towards the door.

It was obvious that what I asked him annoyed him but I still wanted to know.

"Alex doesn't want to tell me," I shouted a bit loudly as I grabbed his shoulder, "And you also don't want to tell me, What are you both hiding from me?"

Drew turned around and made his way towards me then held my chin up to look at him.

"It is just not my secret to tell." He told me with a smile before he turned around and made his way out of the room before I could ask him any further question.

I was left by myself again but that wasn't for too long as Emma seemed to wake up, she was moving in the bed as if troubled.

I quickly made my way towards her. When she noticed me, She was shocked and sat up quickly.

"Don't, You are wounded." I told her softly as I pushed her slowly to lay on the bed but she shook my hands away and glared at me.

"Stay away from me." She yelled at me and made her way to stand up.

When she made her move to stand up, she quickly fell but I quickly caught her in my arms and moved her to sit on the bed again.

I decided to ignore her behavior towards me and be nice towards her, I still didn't know why she hated me.

"Where is Alex?" She asked me as she looked around the room while she let out a hiss of pain.

"He went to fight whoever attacked you I guess" I muttered as I looked at her reaction. Her eyes filled with fear a moment and the next her eyes filled with fury.

"Are you stupid? How can you leave him alone in a situation like his?" She growled at me and I would have stepped back at her tone but being an Alpha's mate, I didn't.

I had enough of her and was about to shout at her to shut the fuck up but she interrupted.

"Those people could kill him" She said slowly.

In the moment, everything around me stopped. I felt like I couldn't breathe. My heart was beating rapidly. I knew Alex was in danger but not in that kind of danger.

I seriously didn't know what happened, I just heard Emma scream and Drew running into the room and telling me to calm down but I couldn't.

All my worries and fear about anything happening to Alex made me shift, Letting my wolf take over and the next thing my wolf was sprinting out of the house and to who knows where but I know that my goal was to reach Alex.

My wolf had completely taken over and I let her.

After running though the forest for a while now and letting the mate bond guide me to Alex. I finally reached a clearing in the middle of the trees and what I saw made me gasp in surprise

Bodies were everywhere surrounded by blood, These people were dead. There were too many of them.

A growl behind me made me turn around to come face to face with Alex's wolf, His wolf was furious as he was. He had some wounds in some parts of his body but I was glad he was alive.

He shifted back and he was standing naked in front of me. He looked amazing. He didn't say anything but after a while, He came towards me and threw a shirt in front of me.

"Shift." He muttered to me in a tone and I could see how impatient he was.

I went behind a tree and shifted. The shirt reached my mid thighs and it had Alex's scent all over which I can't get enough off.

Alex walked closer to me and got a hold of my hand and tugged me to his side.

"Bury the bodies and make sure no other Rogue is in the area, if there are others then send them to me." He shouted to a guy behind him who nodded and quickly left.

His attention went back to me and he looked beyond furious.

"What are you doing here?" He snapped at me.

"Checking to see if you are okay." I told him in a matter of fact as I crossed my arms over my chest.

He chuckled which surprised me, I didn't say anything funny to get that reaction from him.

When he grabbed my chin and forced me to look at him, His eyes were a darker shade.

"Nothing will ever happen to me, Beth" He told me as he ran his hand through my hair softly, "I will never leave you alone, not after I found you, I intend to live an eternity with you and nothing with change that" He continued as he nuzzled my neck and placed a kiss on my mark.

I shivered at his closeness, I just wanted to give myself to him right now. I know things between us are complicated but I didn't care at this moment. I only wanted him.

"Alex I-" I was interrupted as he placed his finger to silence me.

"I told you to stay here but here you are" He nearly shouted at me as he was trying to keep calm, "I don't like you going against everything I say" He muttered as he dragged me along by the arm.

Controlling Alex is back, I felt a little disappointed as our relationship was getting somewhere but of course he had to ruin it.

"I was worried about you." I told his coldly.

"Well nothing happened to me, right?" He replied back arrogantly and I saw him smirk at me.

"You are unbelievable." I huffed as he dragged me to the house where he will tell me that I am not allowed outside, I rolled my eyes at the thought.

"I know that but that is why you are crazy about me" He smirked at my flushed expression. I know there is no point in arguing with him.

I suddenly remembered what I wanted to ask him, it was now or never.

"What happened between you and Emma?" I asked him and I watched his back tense.

His strong jawline tightens, Ad he is clenching his teeth. His eyes had widened and piercing through mine. I cant seem to make out the emotion he could possibly be feeling at this moment.

"It is none of your business" He said angrily and grabbed me roughly as he dragged me again.

"Stop saying that" I told him angrily, I cant take it anymore. He kept things from me and it didn't sit well with me seeing that I am his mate.

"I won't have this conservation with you." He growled at me but I didn't step back at his Alpha tone. I was too determined to know.

"The hell you can't, I waited for you to tell me but you can't even though I am you mate. Maybe I had enough of this, Maybe I should just leave . You keep things from me Alex and I don't like it" I shouted at him and I saw his eyes widen.

By his stiff posture, He seems too uptigh. He was shutting me down.

I grabbed his face in my hands and looked deep in his eyes, I then done the only thing I could think of.

I kissed him.

He was shocked but a second later he was kissing me back. His arms wrapped around my waist and brought me closer to him. It was a soft and passionate kiss which made me shiver as tingles shot through my whole body.

I pulled away and caressed his face softly. He seemed to be lost, like he didn't know what to do.

"Please Alex, talk to me." I pleaded with him and he looked deep in thought.

Alex shakes his head and plants his hands firmly on my hips, staring deep into my eyes, "Give me a moment" He was asking me to him time to get himself together.

I nodded and waited for him to speak.

"I am sorry, Baby. For not telling you before but it isn't something I like to discuss" He said and I was shocked. Alex wasn't the type to apologize and he never apologized to me before and his apology meant so much to me.

"It is okay, You can tell me anything" I told him softly as I placed my head on his chest and wrapped my arms around him. He brings me against his strong muscular body and I press my face in the crook of his neck.

"It is very long and complicated story" He muttered and he looked deep in thought as he started in my eyes.

"What exactly do you want to know about Emma?" He said and I could tell it was hard for him to speak about it.

"Everything about her that you refused to speak about before."

10

CHAPTER 10

I watched how many emotions ram through Alex's eyes, worry, anxious, fear and something else .... i didn't know what it was.He stared at me with that intense look that seemed as he was looking right through me, I shivered at his stare and waited till he spoke."Before i say anything, i don't want you to think badly of me."

Alex said in a low voice, looking at me once before glancing away.I nodded at him and held his hand in mine to reassure him that i would never think badly of him, I know Alex had his cruel and harsh moments sometimes but i never thought badly of him."There was a rogue who entered our pack once," Alex began to say, taking a deep breath,"My dad was going to do the usual punishment to any rogue who entered our pack which was death."I sucked my breath, i knew Alex's pack killed any rogue who entered their pack; i also knew i would be dead now if i wasn't Alex's mate. i signed a huge sight of relief that i am still alive."He was going to kill that rogue but Emma stopped my dad," Alex stopped speaking for a moment and looked at my confused and shocked face,"Turns out that the rogue was her mate."I gasped in shock at the new information, i would have never thought that Emma's mate was a rogue but I guess everything is possible now; since i am Alex's mate and i am also a rogue."My dad accepted him in our pack for the sake of Emma, The pack began to trust him but me and my parents never did, his behaviour was suspicious but we kept it to ourselves seeing how Emma was happy with him."

Alex said slowly as if remembering what happened before and i saw how his eyes turned to a darker shade of black."On a night which i would never forgot, I woke up to some people screaming and i realized one of the people screaming were Emma, I ran to her only to..." He stopped speaking and i could see he was fighting not to cry as one tear ran down his cheek. I quickly pulled him for a comforting hug amd whispered soft words in his ear to calm his down.I waited for a few seconds till he calmed down a little, His body was tense against mine as if he was holding himself back from something.He straightned and looked away from me before he continued,"He slaugh-tered my parents while they were sleeping."I froze as i heard him say these wordsAlex's parents killed by a rogue, no wonder Alex hates them so much and the rogue has no right to kill them this way I looked at him and saw him clenching his jaws, saying he was angry was an understatment; he was furious and he looked ready to kill someone, probably a rogue.

He suddenly looked at me and whispered so lowly that i could barely hear him,"I killed that rogue but not before i tortured him first; that bastard begged me to kill him but i didn't untill he had least expected it, i killed him then.""Emma begged me not kill him, to spare him but i didn't and i blamed all of what happened to our parents on her, i forced her out of the pack because it was her fault that this happened." He told me angrily before he stood up and stormed to who knows where.I stood shocked at my place as i now understood everything, Alex had a rough childhood, that much was obvious but forcing his sister out of the pack; i didn't think it was fair for her, it isn't like she knew her mate was going to commit such a crime.I ran after Alex and when i finally caught up with him, i held his hand and turned to face him but what i saw shocked me.Alex crying! I never saw him crying and i never thought i would see him cry.

Alex and crying in the same sentence just wasn't right.I wiped his tears with my fingers and caressed his face, this seemed to work as he leaned into my hand and inhaled deep ly."Alex, i now understand your cruelty towards the rogues but you can't take out your anger on other innocent people just people of one person." I said in a low whisper as i tried to get my point to him.He stared at me for a while before he shook his head at me."I can't help it, i just feel i want to kill any rogue i encounter." He told me slowly as he ran his hands softly along my arms."I am a rogue and you didn't kill me."

I said softly as i crossed my hands over my chest.He nodded at me before saying,"You are different, you are my mate. I could never think to hurt you, ever." He said softly as he put his head at the crook of my neek and kissed the spot where my mark is, I shivered at his closeness."But still, if i am not your mate; would you have killed me?" I asked, trying to get a reaction from him.I could feel him smirking against my neck as he licked my mark and began to place fierce kisses from my jaw till my neck as his arms wrapped around my waist pulling me tightly against him."No i won't, You are too beautiful; i would have just kept you to myself." He whispered hotly in my ear and i shook my head at him.He always had his way to make me forget about the main subject we were talking about and man was he good at it!His lips met mine in an explosive and passionate kiss, i felt like my breath was stolen from me. it was like every nerve in my body was stolen from me. I couldn't help but kiss him hungrily as he was kissing me. his lips left mine and i groaned in disappoiment but a second later, His lips were on my neck again, biting softly at my mark.

I moaned at him and moved my body closer to him.His hands roamed my body. His hand stopped on my breast and he gave it a squeeze and i moaned in his mouth. I wanted to give myself to him at that moment; nothing matter but him and me, it was like there was nothing around us.I didn't realise he was ripping my shirt except when i heard the sound of fabric being ripped open.

I glared at him but he only smirked at me as he threw the shirt to the floor. I couldn't deny how hot that was.I was now only left in my bra and skirt and under his hungry gaze, his eyes were full of lust as he gazed at me. He looked like he was about to devour me. "I don't want to fight anymore...I know we have a lot to talk about, but I don't have the words right now. Tonight, all I want is you." Alex whispered hotly in my ear and i felt like i was melting.My fingertips scanned all parts of his face. Gently soothing whatever guilt remained in him until Alex was falling for My warm touch. Alex ran his own calloused hands up on my cool smooth legs, and anticipating every goose bump that rose to his touch. My breathing pick up a bit more and He grabbed my thighs before pulling my stomach into his face, and began kissing me. I didn't want it to stop as i pulled His face closer into my skin. the deeper Alex embraced me , the more I didn't mind anymore if he took me right now.

11

CHAPTER 11

Alex carried Elizabeth through the hallways of his house so fast that she felt she would fly if she didn't hold tight to him. They finally reached his bedroom.

With a low growl, Alex quickly swept Elizabeth into his arms, and without parting from her soft lips, he walked toward the massive bed. Elizabeth had her arms wrapped around his neck and Alex groaned when she nibbled gently on his lower lip. He placed one of his hands on her waist and rubbed the flesh for a moment, before he trailed his hand up her side and past her ribs. But before he could touch her covered breast, he moved his hand to her back..

Elizabeth let out a disappointed moan since she had been anticipating his touch on her aching breast. But then she felt him tug at the strings of the top that covered her chest and she tensed slightly before she forced herself to relax.

Alex watched as she blushed endearingly before she moved her hands to cover her breasts either in an involuntary reflex, or because of his hungry gaze. With a small frown he placed his hands over her arms.

"Please down hide from me again, Beth," he told her in a soft yet firm tone, "I enjoy looking at your wonderful breasts."

Elizabeth gave him a small smile as she moved her arms away and placed them gently down at her sides.

How marvelous she looked laying beneath him in nothing but a white piece of cloth that covered where he so desperately wanted to be buried in.

"So beautiful," he whispered as he again leaned down to kiss her.

Elizabeth sighed softly into his mouth before he moved away.

Then he moved down her collarbone, which he bit gently, before moving down the valley of her heaving breasts.

"Alex, oh!" she cried as her fingers threaded into his dark hair, bringing him closer to her chest.

Alex felt his groin tightened as he licked, flicked, and sucked on her lovely nipple while he continued to squeeze her other breast, pinching and rolling the neglected tip between his fingers. He quickly switched breasts and engulfed the other stiff crest in his hot mouth while he grabbed and pushed her other breast up, revealing a glistening peak into the warm air. Elizabeth pushed her chest up so he could have more acces.

With a growl that reflected his delight as much as his relief, Alex buried his face between her breasts and nuzzled them before again sucking on her left dusky tip as he caressed the other breast.

Pulling away, Alex again knelt back and ran his hands leisurely down her sides, past her slim waist, until he rested them on her hips. His fingers played with the edge of her last piece of clothing before he slowly began to tug it down. He saw Elizabeth tense rigidly and he paused, flicking his eyes up to see her staring at him with wide, nervous eyes.

"It's okay," he murmured reassuringly, "Relax."

Elizabeth swallowed thickly as Alex again tugged at her undergarment. Her body stiffened even further as he pulled it down her hips and her breathing increased as he slid it down her legs. She felt her face heat up as he held the small white clothing in his hands, stared at the damp spot heatedly for a moment, before tossing it over the bed like he had done to her top wrap.

Alex's eyes quickly darted to the place he had wished so many times to gaze upon and feel surrounding his thick length.

Of all the women, assembled together, she was the most beautiful.

"So beautiful," he whispered huskily and he smiled when he saw her relax and her eyes brighten.

12

CHAPTER 12

The first thing I became aware of as I slowly drifted up from the depths of slumber was Alex's warm hands moving over my skin, bringing a pleasure that made my entire body melt. In my still foggy mind, i realized Alex was hovering over me by the warmth and light weight of his body touching mine.

"Mm," I moaned softly when his fingers slowly trailed down my side.

As if knowing that he had succeeded in waking her up, Alex's soft touches became more firm and adventurous.

"Good morning," I heard him greet huskily.

"It's morning already?" I muttered giving out a soft yawn before finally deciding to open my eyes.

I saw Alex looking down at me with a smile and gleaming golden eyes before I allowed my gaze to sweep the room as my drowsiness began to leave me.

"It's barely dawn!" I almost whined as another yawn escaped me.

I felt more than heard Alex chuckle and I glanced back at him with a halfhearted glare.

"Mm," Alex murmured in pleasure. "They say the mornings can be the best time to make love," he commented with a wolfish grin.

With that said, he bucked his hips slowly and I gasped in shock when i felt him harden inside me, reminding me that we had fallen asleep with our bodies connected intimately. i felt myself blush along with the rest of my body as my core immediately clenched in need.

"What you say about the mornings is a pretense because it doesn't seem matter to you the hour or the place," i retorted playfully.

"You know me so well, love," he responded with a chuckle.

"Shouldn't you be with the pack?" I asked him before wrapping my arms around his neck.

"No, I am exactly where I need to be right now." He whispered before pulling me into his arms.

"If you have to go then go," I said but deep down, I wanted him to hold me today and never leave but I know he had duties since he was the alpha.

"I have a duty as your mate and I just want to stay with you." He said firmly and I snuggled deeper into his chest.

After making love another time, Alex had to leave; he said it was something urgent but he refused to tell me.

I hoped that after yesterday, he would be able to tell me everything but obviously he didn't, but at least he told me about his sister and I know with time he would be able to tell me anything.

Drew was lounging in one of the sofas downstairs. He was playing xbox and he was really focused on it.

I went down and sat next to him and he turned his head to look at me, He smirked and raised his eyebrows at me as if telling me a secret message.

"What?" I said confused by his silence.

"Why did you wake up so late?" He said before a grin took over his face.

"I was tired," I replied, and quickly distracted my gaze some-where else, away from his gaze.

"Uh huhh." He muttered, when I turned to face him, he was waggling his eyebrows at me.

I felt the blush coming again so I went to the kitchen as I was hungry anyway.

"Where is Emma?" I asked as I finally realized she wasn't here, I knew she was rude to me last time we talked but I understood her reasons.

She was worried about Alex; Alex was the only family left for her and even if they had arguments, they cared about each other.

"Went to the mall, I guess." Drew shrugged as he made his way towards the kitchen.

"What are you making?" He asked and I looked at him, I realized that he hadn't slept because he looked exhausted.

"Bacon." I muttered before making my way towards him and looking close at him.

There was something bothering him, it was that obvious.

Before I can my mouth to ask him what is bothering him, He raised his hands as if to silence me.

"I know what you are going to say and the answer is I am fine" He muttered before running his hand through his hair.

I crossed my arms over my chest and glared at him, I knew he was hiding something.

"Fine but no bacon for you." I smirked at him as I continued to make lunch and I could hear his sharp intake of breath behind me, I silently chuckled.

"What?!" He yelled as he raised his hands in the air ,"You know that isn't fair!"

"It is fair for me." I told him, before turning back to the food that I was cooking.

Drew groaned at my words before finally nodding.

"I am not sick but I don't know what the hell is wrong with me, my wolf had been on edge since yesterday but I cant know why." He said before turning his head to the side.

"Do you think it is because you are near your mate." I asked as I heard it before, maybe his mate was near and I knew whoever she is; she would be lucky to have someone as Drew.

"I don't know but I don't care." He told me before looking at me and nodding towards the food, "is the food ready?" He asked and It was clear he was trying to avoid the subject.

I decided to let it drop for now since I didn't want to annoy him further, Drew should be happy since probably he would find his mate.

But he didn't seem that happy, I knew Drew was the ladies man and was still is. I hoped when he found his mate, he will change for the better.

We sat in the dinning room, eating and I laughed as Drew recalled old memories from his past.

"Being Elizabeth's guard everyday, what a privilege." He smirked as he rolled his eyes.

"You should feel lucky you are hanging with me, I am cool." I replied annoyed by him.

Drew started laughing really hard and my frown deepened at his reaction.

He was about to replay but suddenly stopped before his face grew serious and he stood up.

"I have to leave." He said quickly before making his way towards the door.

First Alex then him, something was wrong.

"Drew you aren't leaving until you tell me what is wrong." I said as moved in front of him to block his way

"Elizabeth, as much as I would love to stay with you, I have to go." He said before picking me up bridal style like I weighted nothing and went towards the sofa and placed me there.

Before I knew it, he was out of the door; before realizing what I was doing I ran behind him and followed him.

Surprisingly he didn't went far, he went to the little room in the garden where .....

Alex tortured anyone who entered his pack, mainly rogues. I remembered the last time I went there, Alex snapped the neck of a man from my group in front of my eyes.

Everything in me was telling me to go but as curious I was, I went and stood before the door.

There were someone shouting and something laughing. I could that It was Alex shouting but the person laughing was unknown to me.

Before I could lose my courage, I entered and suddenly all eyes in the room were on me. Alex stared at me and he was trembling with rage, his body was shaking with anger.

Maybe it was a bad decision after all to come here.

Then I made the mistake of looking behind me, all of the blood drained from my face, and my heart nearly stopped. Nothing other than confusion and silence, embracing myself for the worst. I felt like I was imagining things but I knew that everything around me now was real. There chained to the chair with silver which obviously was hurting him and his wolf. Blood were everywhere on his clothes and blood ran from his nose and his nose was broken, he was a mess and I am sure the reason of this was because of Alex. I could only utter only one word.

"Dad"

13

— • —

CHAPTER 13

With my hand I grabbed the doorway to keep myself upright, I felt that if I didn't; I will surely fall on the ground. I didn't see my dad for 8 years and I never expected to see him again, ever. I didn't think he would have the courage to come and see us after what he has done to me and my mother.

We were rogues because of him, because he betrayed our pack then escaped. The pack wanted to blame someone after all and they blamed us and kicked us out of the pack. I was 10 at that time, I was young and still hadn't shifted. My mum had to provide for us by herself and I could always see the sadness on her face because of what her mate had done.

She was heartbroken and she didn't like to show it but I saw how sad she was; this was one of the reasons why I didn't want a mate before but now Alex was my everything and I can't imagine a life without him.

All eyes were on me, Alex's eyes were wide in surprise and he shook his head in disbelief. Drew raised his eyebrows at me as if I was joking and my dad looked between Alex and me with pure resentment and hatred. I was so confused and bewildered as to where all that hatred was coming from. I am the one who should be looking at him like that for what he had done but he was looking at me like I am the one at fault here.

"Elizabeth, he is your father?" Alex asked as he walked slowly towards me and I could see from his face that he hoped the answer would be no.

"Yes." I said in a low whisper as I looked at the ground.

I didn't need to look into Alex's eyes to see they were full of disappointment.

I heard Alex chuckle and I looked up at him to see him smiling evilly at me as his eyes changed to a dark colour that made me scared at what he was about to do.

In a minute, Alex had my dad on the floor and he was on top of him. Alex punched his face over and over again. I winced at the crunching sound as the fist and face connected.

If Alex didn't stop now, my dad will surely die and I couldn't allow that. I know me and my mother suffered a lot because of him but he was still my father and a part in me still loved him.

Without thinking what to do, I bent down and grabbed Alex's hand to stop him from punching. Unfortunately, Alex didn't look back and see who grabbed him. He just pushed his arm back and it came back hitting me hard in my jaw.

I was thrown back from the hard hit. My eyes filled with tears and I couldn't think straight because of the pain in my jaw.

"Elizabeth!" Drew yelled as he came running towards me and grabbed my chin to check if there was anything serious.

Alex finally looked behind him and his eyes grew wide as he saw who he had hit. Before I knew it, he had me in his lap and whispered words of how sorry he was.

"I didn't know it was you, I am so sorry! shit I swear I didn't mean to do that." Alex told me and I could hear the sorrow in his voice. I nodded to him as I rested my head on his chest.

"Drew, take her to the house and get her some ice." Alex told Drew in his alpha voice as he stood up and carried me bridal style and handed me to Drew who quickly carried me and went to leave.

"I missed you so much, Elizabeth! how is your mother, still suffering because of me?" My father said as he laughed.

I was about to go and punch him myself but the sickening sound of bones breaking was heard as Alex punched him in the face and the next thing I saw before Drew left the room was my dad falling to the ground, unconscious.

I winced as Drew placed ice on my jaw, I snatched it from him as I glared at him but he only chuckled at my reaction.

Putting the ice back on my jaw, i tried to block the pain but it was nearly impossible because it hurt a lot.

"Why was Alex torturing him?" I asked Drew as that question has been nagging me for a while now.

Drew looked at me as if deciding whether to tell me or not.

"Your father is the leader of a big group of rogues, around 200 and they aren't what you call... friendly." Drew told me slowly as he regarded any reaction from me.

I was really confused now, I knew my dad was a rogue now because he ran away from the pack but I didn't knew he was the leader of a whole group of rogues.

"I am also from a group of rogues, you know." I told him as I placed the ice on the counter and went to sit down.

"For one, your group never attacked anyone or even tried to attack a pack before, I know some of you enter the packs to get a few things" He smirked at me and I blushed as I remembered that I had done this before knowing Alex was my mate.

"But none of you are as them." Drew finished and I nodded at him, I know there were rogues who done terrible things to other packs.

That is why people hated rogues but there were also good ones but they were so few that people didn't take notice of them.

I twirled a strand of my hair as I thought of the next question to ask him.

"I understand, but Alex looked more than furious when hitting my dad, like there is something between them." I told Drew and he nodded.

"It is about Alex's parents, you see-" Before he could continue, there was knocking on the door.

I was about to stand but Drew quickly walked towards the door and opened it and there was a woman standing there who looked my age. She had blonde hair that reached her waist, green eyes and she was average height.

I noticed she looked mad, well furious to be honest. Before I could ask who was she, Her fist connected with Drew's mouth.

I watched as Drew spit out blood. I looked at her, angrily as I stormed towards her; probably to knock some sense into her, she can't just go around hitting people.

Drew blocked my way and shook his head at me, I looked at him like he was crazy. Defending her after she hit him like that.

"What? Cat ate your tongue!" She growled at him and was about to hit him again but I grabbed her hand and pushed her away.

"Who the hell are you?" I yelled at her, I didn't know who she was but I knew she was crazy to attack the beta of the pack who could kill her in a minute.

She looked at me for a while with hatred and if I wasn't mistaken jealousy before she turned her gaze at Drew who looked at her with guilt.

"You were avoiding me because of her! I hope she is worth it." She told him in a voice filled with venom before she spun around and left the house.

I shook my head at what happened, this day couldn't get any worse. i didn't know why she came and what confused me more was why did Drew defend her. She hit him and I guessed he would have done something but he didn't, it will like he knew he deserved it.

I looked at Drew and he looked broken, like something terrible happened and caused him to be like this.

"Drew, what-" I was interrupted as he looked into my eyes and they were filled with sorrow and sadness that made my heart ache for him.

"She is my mate." Drew told me as if knowing my question.

I guess I know now why Drew looked troubled earlier today, he found his mate but why she was acting like this and why Drew avoiding her was a mystery to me but I was going to ask Drew.

I also figured out something, Alex wasn't here. He should have come when he heard the yelling but he didn't. I swallowed nervously as I felt that whatever he was doing has something to do with my father.

14

CHAPTER 14

"Elizabeth?"

My eyes were closed, I tried opening my eyes but it was hard. I had a headache and I felt like I couldn't move.

"Come on baby, wake up." A soft, husky voice whispered in my ears and I felt fingers caressing my cheek.

Alex

I tied to wake up, open my eyes or make any sound but I was unable to even utter one word. I panicked and sat up quickly but the pounding in my head increased as I let out a whimper while holding my head.

Arms wrapped about my body as he pushed me down on the bed and ran his hand through my hair, his eyes were full of concern worry and guilt.

What happened to me?

Waking up feeling disoriented, any move made the pounding in my head increase and it took a great effort to open my eyes.

Finally it clicked, I was drugged and I already know who did it, judging by the guilt look in his eyes, then I decided to do something which I didn't regret.

The sound of the slap echoed throughout the bedroom.

Alex's head turned to the side but when he looked at me, his eyes were narrowed and he went to grab me.

I moved away from him, I was furious now. I know Alex did horrible things and I have forgiven him but I couldn't take the idea of someone drugging me and the fact that it was my mate who did it.

"Why did you do it?" I asked shakily as I looked at him, I didn't need to tell him what 'it' is because I am sure he understood.

His eyes held so much remorse and guilt that I felt bad for him.

Stop it Elizabeth! he is just acting to make you forgive him

He crouched in front of me and reached for me.

"Stay away." I punched him in the chest , my fists hitting him over and over again.

He held me by the shoulders, eyes never leaving my face, he didn't move as I continued my assault on him until I was exhausted. I fell backward, my fists throbbing. I was about to slap him again but he grabbed my wrist.

"Once I will take but not twice." He told me as he shook his head. When I relaxed my arm, he let me go.

"We need to talk about this." He said firmly and I know there is no point in arguing with him.

I didn't want him anywhere near me now but I wanted to know the reason he drugged me. I finally nodded to him to explain.

"There was a bloodbath, Elizabeth." He told me then ran his hand through his hair, something that he does when he frustrated about something.

"Between who?" I asked slowly as I was trying to process that there was a bloodbath, which was strange because the last thing I remember was Drew's mate who left and me talking to Drew and then he gave me a drink.

The drink must have something in it because I was sure that whatever was in the drink made me drunk and I also knew that Alex mind linked Drew to do it but that didn't stop my anger towards Drew now.

"Our pack and your father's group." He said darkly, his voice was full of venom and he looked ready to murder someone.

I didn't forgot about my father, I just wished I would never hear or see him again but I knew it won't be that easy since my father has something to do with Alex's parents.

"Is anyone hurt?" I told him, my voice was now shaky as I was worried that anyone got hurt from the pack. I didn't have the best relationship with the pack but that was because I didn't get anytime to be with them; mainly because too many things happened.

Alex's eyes turned darker and he began to shook in fury. He was going to shift, that much was obvious.

I reached for him and pulled him in a hug. He wasted no time in wrapping his hands around me and kept inhaling my scent, I could feel him calming down.

"What happened, Alex?" I titled my head to look at him, his eyes were glassy but hard.

"They helped him escape before I could finally have my revenge." He growled pulling away from me, he stood up and began to pace.

I know he was talking about my dad, Alex held a grudge against him; I just don't know why but I intended to find out.

"What did my father do?" I asked calmly.

Alex turned to me, he was furious now. His eyes were blazing and they contained too much hate and anger.

"Your father was the one who ordered my parent's death." He snarled, the anger that swarmed around him thickly scared me, he was fuming. I decided to remain quiet and keep it safe.

I know my father did horrible things but I didn't expect him to do something that horrible. i understood now why Alex, wanted no needed to kill him, he wanted revenge. If Alex wanted revenge then I won't stop him.

My father and his group killed innocent people from different packs and that is why people hated rogues. I just didn't know that my dad was the leader of a whole group of them; I thought one day he will come back and apologize but apparently he was busy, killing another people.

"Alex, I am sorry." I said softly as I went to him and hugged him. He looked like he was going to go wolf now. His black eyes turned to me. His canines were out and his claws were extracted.

"Calm down." I said softly as I tightened my hold on him, I needed to calm him down. I nestled my head in his skin, blowing my breath softly against his ear.

"Elizabeth." Alex growled breathlessly.

Alex's hold on my waist was so tight. I felt him calming down which I was thankful for. His canines were no longer out but his claws were and they ripped the clothes which I was wearing.

"I am sorry for that, I never imagined he could do something like this." I told him and I could feel him walking to the bed. He sat down and brought me over his lap, pressing me closer to his chest.

"I need to find him, I won't stop till i do and then i will kill him and each one of his group slowly and I will enjoy their pain." He said darkly.

I shivered, I didn't like when Alex talked like this. I know I should get used to it by now but still it scared me.

"Why did you drug me, Alex?" I asked him firmly, taking his face between my hands.

"I told you there was a bloodbath." He said, looking at me as if he was helping a child to understand.

"I know that but why? I could have helped!" I practically yelled. "Don't you tell me because it was dangerous and all that nonsense, I can defend myself." I told him defiantly, trying to stand up.

Alex smirked inwardly but he held his grip for me.

"Elizabeth, try to understand." He told me softly, " I know you can defend yourself but I will be busy fighting to keep an eye on you." He lifted my chin and I met his eyes, " I will never forgive myself if something happened to you."

I touched his cheek, he always managed to calm me down when I am angry at him.

"But what if something happened to you and I wasn't there to help you." I told him.

"Nothing will happen to me; I am the alpha and nothing can touch me except you." He smirked at me when I blushed.

"Promise you will never drug me again because I swear if you-" I was silenced when he placed his hand on my mouth.

"I won't do it again because I can't take it when you are angry at me but you are still not joining any fight." He ordered in his alpha voice.

I was about to argue but he suddenly stood up.

"Come with me, I have to show you something that will make up for what I had done." He gave me a dazzling smile.

I wondered what it was and I found myself walking towards him. He grabbed my hand and began walking downstairs.

Once I reached downstairs, I looked around but there was nothing. I looked at Alex whose eyes were lit in amusement as he watched my confusion.

"Go to the backyard." He told me, smiling at me which made me more anticipated to what he wanted to show me.

I walked there and once I reached it, I gasped. I couldn't believe it and I couldn't describe my happiness.

Standing there was my mum, smiling at me. She opened her arms and I wasted no time in running towards her and wrapping my arms around her.

I missed her so much, I knew she was worried about me and I hated to be the cause of it. Just being in her arms brought peace to me, all trouble seemed far away from me now and I just wanted to stay in her arms.

"Mum, I missed you." I said breathlessly and I could feel tears running down my cheeks.

"I know, I was worried about you; I thought something happened to you." She told me and I could feel her tightening her hold on me.

"I am here now and I am fine." I told her, pulling away from her. I smiled at her and brushed my tears away.

"Yes and we have a fine young alpha to thank for that." My mum said, looking behind me. I turned around and saw Alex, standing there. He was smiling at me as he watched us.

"Thank you." I told him. I didn't expect Alex to do that at all, I felt my love for him growing; I was thankful he was my mate. He was my world and I know entering his pack was the best thing I had ever done because I got to meet him.

"Anything for you." He told me softly and I could see the love in his eyes, for me. I was lucky I had him.

I saw Drew coming behind him and he told him something quietly. Alex frowned before nodding.

"I have to go but no one is allowed outside of the house." He said seriously before turning around and leaving. Drew followed behind him immediately without sparing me another glance.

I was afraid now, I know something happened and I hoped Alex would be okay. Drew also ignored me like I wasn't there, I swallowed as I suspected he was angry at me. I was, in a way, a reason of the problem with his mate but I didn't know why as I didn't do anything.

Alex, take care of yourself. I will be waiting for you when you come back.

I mind linked him and almost immediately he replied.

I will but don't go out, I have 3 of my men around the house so don't bother trying to come; I need you safe, love

I signed as he was so protective of me, it troubled me several time but I wasn't angry at him, I could only hope nothing bad will happen to him. I knew Alex was one of the strongest alphas in the country and no one liked to mess with him but I was still worried about him.

I felt that there are always trouble but I know one day we will overcome them and then he would be finally able to leave in peace, me and Alex, I wished it will be soon.

15

Chapter 15

"**S**o tell me how have you been?" My mum voice's made me turn my head towards her. I wasn't aware of the frown on my face but my mum noticed.

She walked towards me and hugged me. I could feel she was trying to reassure me but it didn't help.

There was something wrong, I felt it.

"I have to go to Alex." I said suddenly, looking at her to see her shake her head at me.

"You can't," She said as she smiled at me before grabbing my hand, "There is a serious problem now, Alex didn't take you because it was dangerous and I can't let you out; you may get hurt."

I already know that I might get hurt but what if something happened to Alex, I wouldn't be there to help him.

"I am sorry but I have to go." I told her, with determination in my eyes and I could tell that she saw it because she didn't argue with me.

"Take care of yourself," She said as she hugged me tightly before whispering in my ear ,"If you saw your father, don't ever trust him. He won't stop at nothing to kill Alex now even if it meant hurting you."

I gasped as I looked at her eyes and in that moment, I knew she sensed my father was here, Mate bond. I could see the hurt in her eyes even though she was trying to hide it.

"I already know that." Except for the fact that he wanted to kill Alex now and probably me if I stood in his way.

Clenching my hands into fists, I tried to calm myself down. My father was the cause of all these problems. He ruined my life when I was young but I vowed to myself that I will stop him from doing it again.

Running out of the front door, my way was blocked by 2 men and I forget that Alex had put some of his men around the house.

"Luna, is there something wrong?" A man, a whole foot taller than me, said with concern in his voice.

What can I say now? I am going to save my mate! They would never let me out, I am sure of that.

I shook my head before smiling politely and closing the door. I could see the look of confusion in his eyes and I didn't blame him.

I ran upstairs to my room and opened the window, remembering how I jumped from it to escape from Alex, only now I am doing it to save Alex. I chuckled at the thought.

Before thinking any further, I jumped down and looked around for any other men but I was glad as i saw no one standing around.

I was about to shift to my wolf when I heard the sound of sobbing, walking forward to the source of sound, I gasped in surprise.

Drew's mate was running towards me, crying uncontrollably. Once she reached me, she signed in relief.

"You are here." She said more to herself than me. I didn't feel like replaying to her actually. Our last encounter didn't go that well and to say she was rude was an understatement.

I could tell she sensed that I didn't want to talk to her because the next thing her eyes were full of guilt and shame. I expected she was going to apologize or something but I was wrong.

"Where is Drew? something happened to him, I feel it." She said alarmed as she looked around her before her eyes settled on me, she was panicked as I was.

"He went with Alex, there is something going on and I was just going there." I told her before running towards the forest.

My heart no longer feels it is inside my chest since I felt like I couldn't breathe. I was overwhelmed. Now I knew that something was truly wrong, I felt the tears running down my cheeks as I thought of what could have happened.

I was jerked out of my thoughts when a hand came down on my shoulder and i saw Drew's mate standing there, looking at me seriously.

"I am coming with you." She told me and I could tell she was serious.

I opened my mouth to tell her that she may get hurt and Drew wouldn't be so happy about it but she held her hand to silence me.

"I am coming whether you like it or now and," She sighs, rolling her eyes at me ,"I can protect myself and I am sorry for last time, I misjudged you."

I managed a small smile before nodding at her to tell her that she was forgiven.

Without wasting anymore time, I sprinted towards the forest, hoping that mate bond could tell me the way to Alex quickly. Behind me I could hear Drew's mate running behind me.

Hang on Alex, I am coming.

We reached the area of the fight, I could hear wolves growling and flesh ripping. Dead bodies lay on the floor.

I swallowed thickly as I looked around, that was my father's fault and his group of rogues. Innocent people were dead protecting this pack but taking a second look, most who died were rogues because I never saw them around here.

"What are you doing here?" Someone growled behind me, I was about to shift to protect myself but calmed down when I saw it was just Drew.

His nose was bleeding and there a long gash at his side which was also bleeding.

"What happened to you?" I told him shakily, not the bit scared from the look in his eyes. He was angry but I was worried about him.

"Drew!" A voice suddenly yelled before his mate hugged him from behind and he immediately groaned in pain.

The pain became his least concern as he whipped around and locked eyes with her; he suddenly became furious and his eyes turned to a dark shade.

"What the fuck are you two doing here, go back!" He growled which made me shiver, he was scaring me, I have to admit.

I never saw him angry and to have seen it wasn't something I wanted to see again. He was glaring at me and her but his eyes finally settled at me.

"You brought Lucy here, didn't you?" He demanded, his question so full of accusation and I know he was blaming me.

"I-" I began to defend myself before Lucy came and stood next to me, crossing her arms.

"She tried to stop me from coming here but I came anyway because I was worried about you." She told him, glaring at him.

Her words didn't effect him that much because he was still upset with me.

"You never listen to Alex, do you?" He said , still shaking from anger.

"What did i ever do to you?" I yelled at him.

"You are putting your life in danger as well as my mate and that isn't supposed to make angry, is it?" He asked sarcastically.

By now a few tears escaped my eyes. That was it, I shifted to my wolf and ran towards the sounds of the fight, ignoring him as he shouted for me to stop.

Alex where are you?

"Elizabeth, thought you would get rid of me?"

I turned around to look at my father with that evil smile on his face, I growled at him but he only laughed.

"I can't find Alex, do you have any idea where he is?" He asked, expecting an answer as if I would tell him.

I thumped my paws on the ground and growled at him to go away from here but he only reached inside to pull a gun.

A gun wouldn't be able to hurt a werewolf but at closer expectation, I took a step back. It was a gun but I was sure it had silver bullets in it. The most serious thing that hurt werewolfs; Silver and in some cases it killed them.

Elizabeth, hang on I am coming but you will regret going against my orders and leaving the house

Alex mind linked me, I felt relief at the knowledge that Alex was fine but I didn't care that a gun was pointed at me in this second. All that mattered was that Alex was safe and I couldn't allow him to come here.

You can't come-

I was stopped as the sound of gun shot echoed through the forest but I didn't feel anything at all. I looked up to see the look of shock on my dad's face before looking down to see Alex's wolf there.

I felt my heart stop beating as I shifted back. I felt like that a part of me was dying. I crawled to Alex's side. Once I was there, He shifted slowly to his human form.

He was dying, I began sobbing uncontrollably as I pulled his head to my lap. I felt like dying, it was my fault he was here, hurt and close to death. I shouted angrily and rested my head on his shoulder and let myself drown in sorrow which without a doubt will be forever, that if I didn't die first.

"Alex, wake up." I told him as I shook his shoulder. He couldn't leave me, especially not when everything between us was starting to be great. He was my mate and I couldn't imagine my life without him.

I looked at the spot where my dad was, only to find it empty. He got what he wanted and then he escaped. I saw red and vowed that I will get revenge soon.

I looked back at Alex and held his hand, running my hand through his hair.

"Don't leave me Alex please." I cried as I lost all hope.

Out of nowhere, his hand held mine as he opened open his eyes. I never felt so happy in my entire life and I kissed him all over his face and hugged him tightly as more tears sprang to my eyes but this time it was tears of joy.

"Elizabeth." He rasped as he painfully raised his arm to grab onto my hand. "Are you okay?"

"I am fine, Alex..." My voice trembled before I scowled at him. "Stupid! Why did you take that bullet, it was meant for me."

Alex frowned as he squeezed my hand and I looked to his eyes.

"I would rather die than allow anyone or anything to harm you." He told me fervently.

I couldn't help but lunge myself at him as he hissed at pain, I pulled away mumbling a sorry.

"Careful, Elizabeth! I was just shot. You have to handle me with care." Alex lightly teased an I laughed.

"You are going to be okay." I told him softly as I ran my fingers through his dark hair.

"When I am okay, I won't be forgetting your punishment, sweetheart." He smirked at me when I frowned at him and I know he meant it.

"We have to get out that bullet from you." I told him as I stood up, I had to take him to pack's doctor to get that bullet out of him. I wasn't sure just how as I couldn't carry him alone and he appeared to be fighting unconscious.

"Alex." Drew yelled as came running towards us.

I now know just how. I didn't dare to look at Drew as I briefly told him what happened. He carried Alex who was by now unconscious and we headed back to the pack.

"Elizabeth, I am sorry-" He began to say but I shook my head at him.

"Save it, I don't want to hear it." After I uttered those words, I wished I could take them back as hurt suddenly flushed in his eyes and he looked down but right now I didn't want to speak to him.

I hoped we arrive to the pack quickly to take the bullet out of Alex, Alex body weakened every minute the bullet stayed in him so that was why he was unconscious but he will live. The thought made me relax. I couldn't imagine my life without him in it; I stopped thinking about the subject since it only brought me pain.

I focused instead on a bright future with him but that won't happen until my father is stopped. I was going to help Alex bring him and the rogues with him down, I hoped that we would be able to do it soon so we could continue our lives without attacks and troubles.

16

— • —

CHAPTER 16

While the pack doctor checked Alex's body, I laid there and held his hand. He had been unconscious for 2 days now and I hardly left his side. I couldn't think of anything else but Alex and when he is going to wake up.

My mum tried to reassure that he was going to be okay and even tried to convince to get some rest but I couldn't leave his side.

Lucy even showed up and tried to cheer me up and I appreciated her presence; I began to like her company a lot. She told me Drew was sorry and that he was just worried but I knew he made a mistake so I just smiled at her and shook my head.

"Luna, he may wake in the next few hours." The pack doctor said with a smile on his face.

I restrained myself from jumping and dancing in the room. I and my wolf ached for his presence; also the guilt that it was my fault didn't help it. I was stupid to just go there when I knew Alex could take care of himself but I couldn't stop myself.

"Thank you for taking care of him." I told him and I meant it.

"It is just my job and there is no pack without an alpha to look after it." He said before leaving the room and I just stared after him.

It was obvious how everyone in the pack respected and loved Alex, he was everything a pack could ask for and I heard many of the pack say he is the best alpha so far.

I snuggled into Alex's side and laid my head on his chest, I almost whimpered when he didn't wrap his hand around me. I have been waiting for him to talk to me, embrace me and tell me everything is going to be okay for 2 days and I was more than glad to know he is going to wake up soon.

"Alex, please wake up. I need you here with me." I whispered in his ear before kissing his cheek.

"Elizabeth. You need to rest! This isn't good for you." Lucy told me, entering the room, while raising her hands to demonstrate her point.

"He is going to wake up in a few hours and I want to be here when he wakes up." I said sharply before looking back at Alex. When are you going to wake up Alex?

Lucy walked over and gave me pleading eyes. "I consider you now as my friend and I am to look after you. You better suck it up and get up now because you need to rest for a while."

I glanced at Alex one time and I willingly accepted Lucy's hand and she led me to the kitchen and I saw her prepare something for me to eat.

Just a shower and sleep for an hour then I will go back.

With it, I smiled at her and was about to thank her when my eyes noticed the mark at her neck. I sucked a breath, how didn't I notice it before.

Drew marked her and I didn't believe it happened so fast when just 3 days they had a problem with each.

"He marked you?" I asked with a smirk and she immediately blushed, looking anywhere but me.

"Yes," She sighed as she touched the mark before meeting my eyes. "He just done it all of sudden, he didn't even ask! He just did it like I had no opinion in it." She growled and I could see she was angry.

"You aren't the only one actually whose mate is like this." I gnawed at my buttom lips.

I remembered how Alex marked me the first day I came here, I was so angry at him. I even attempted to escape from him.

I smiled at the memory; we had came a long way since then and I was happy for it. I was glad my escape attempt failed because if it did succeed, I know I wouldn't be here right now with Alex.

"I know what you mean, it is no wonder they are cousins." Lucy sighed as she went on to prepare the rest of the food.

I gasped at what she said, Alex and Drew cousins; I knew they were best friends but cousins. Alex never told me.

Lucy appeared to have noticed the frown on my face before she gave me a smile.

"Drew also didn't tell me." She told me and I was amused at how well she could read me.

"Why didn't they just tell us?" I asked, biting my lower lip, anxious for the answer.

"I don't know actually, maybe they just didn't want to." She said while crossing her arms over chest, clearly thinking about something.

"Who told you anyway?" I asked. Whoever that person must know Alex well.

"Emma, she is his-" She began to say but I interrupted her.

"Sister, we met a few times. How do you know her?" My curiosity was growing by the minute now.

"We were friends at high school then she just disappeared and I actually never saw her again." She told me and she looked in deep though as if remembering something.

That must by the time Alex's parents died, he blamed her and kicked her out of the pack. I thought people know but apparently no one did.

I nodded at her, not wanting to speak further in this discussion. The fact that neither Alex nor Drew told me before hurts but I was reassured by the idea they must had a reason.

"I am tired, I will go to sleep for a while." I told her standing up and making my way upstairs and I could hear her protesting.

I wasn't tired but I missed Alex, I left his side only 10 minutes ago but I ached to be next to him and never leave him.

I didn't realize I had fallen asleep until someone grabbed my arms. I almost flinched if it wasn't for the hand running through my hair.

Alex

"Hello sleepyhead, took you long enough to wake up." He smirked at me while stretching. I couldn't help myself; I just lunged at him and he caught me while chuckling.

"Alex, you are finally awake." I inhaled his scent, I could feel myself and my wolf relax finally; knowing that our mate is awake.

"Have I slept this long?" He asked, while running his hand through his hair, making it look messier and sexy.

"2 days and they couldn't go any slower." I smiled at him when he chuckled. His black eyes met mine.

He was awake. Alive and well and he spoke to me.

"Why are you crying?" He asked in a concerned voice.

I touched my cheeks to release that I was indeed crying but what he didn't know was that those tears were tears of joy because he was well and awake.

Before I could blink, he had me on his lap and wiped my cheeks with his thumb before inhaling my scent.

"What happened? Are you okay? Did anyone hurt you because I swear I will-" I silenced him by kissing him fiercely.

Alex groaned loudly against my mouth, he pulled me even closer to himself until I was flushed against him. Grabbing my buttom with his hand, he drew me closer to him. I pulled away from him because I could feel it was leading somewhere else.

As much as I wanted to, Lucy was in the house and she may come looking for me again; I blushed at the thought.

Alex frowned and tried to grab me again but I stood up, giggling at his expression while shaking my head at him.

"Why? I do think I deserve another kiss for saving your live." He smirked at me and I shook my head at him.

"Drew's mate is in the house." I told him and I could see his frown depended.

"I am fine now so she can leave." He growled as he moved to stand up but I stopped him.

"Alex, stop being rude." I frowned at him, i could see he was trying to control himself from going downstairs and telling her to leave.

"It isn't rude to want my mate all to myself." He whispered hotly in my ear. I made the mistake of looking down at his hard abs. I wanted to touch them; they looked so delicatable.

"Changed your mind already?" His voice snapped me back to reality and I shook my head to rid my head of all the dirty thoughts.

"Nope." I said and smiled in victory when he frowned.

"Fine when she leaves." He huffed and went to grab a shirt which I was glad for.

I walked towards him but stopped when his eyes suddenly met mine. He moved closer to me and kept inhaling my scent.

What was he doing?

I thought he was trying to seduce me which led me to take a step back because I know that If I didn't move away now, I would give in.

"Don't move." He growled and his arms around me tightened. He looked deep in thought.

After what seemed like forever, he looked at me. He was smirking and his eyes held love, desire, happiness and appreciation.

"What is there, Alex?" I asked and I could hear my voice shaking, there was something. I just wasn't sure if it was good or not.

He caressed my cheeks while staring into my eyes. "You know I love you more than life itself, if anything happened to you, I wouldn't be able to go on living, don't you?"

I nodded and he meant the life for me as well, He was everything to me and I do know that I won't be able to live if anything to him.

"I would do anything for you, just ask for it. You are my everything; my entire world and you know that I would never let anything happen to you, I would rather die than you getting hurt." He whispered in my ear and my heart swelled with love for him.

He was too good for me, sometimes I think I didn't deserve him but I was glad he was my mate and I was thankful for it. He had shown me he loved me in so different ways which made me love him even more than I already did.

"I love you too, Alex. I can't imagine my life without you and I plan for us to live happily together for a long time. I know we always have troubles but I know we are able to overcome them like we will overcome anything bad in the future." I told him and I meant every word I said.

He nuzzled my neck and licked my mark at my neck, he bit at the flesh there and I moaned, wrapping my arms around his neck. He whispered in my ear softly that I almost didn't hear him.

"Elizabeth, You are pregnant."

17

CHAPTER 17

Alex's POV

Elizabeth is looking at me like she didn't believe what I just said, she shook her head at me and I didn't miss the way her body was trembling.

Her lip quivered when she noticed that I wasn't kidding. Carefully I directed her towards the sofa where she collapsed.

"Rest for a minute, sweety. We will talk later." I told her softly before taking a place next to her.

A soft sob escapes her and it rips through me. I pull her on my lap where I shower her face with kisses to calm her down.

"Are you sure?" She mumbles as she stares into my eyes.

"Positive." That one word was enough for her to break down crying again in front of me.

I didn't like her reaction, at all. When I sniffed the air around her; I noticed she was pregnant and I felt like I was the happiest man alive. I wished I can show her that she didn't need to fear anything, I will protect her at any cost.

"We have too many problems to deal with, it isn't the right time." She said sharply as she started to stand up but I held her in place.

"I know but I don't see the problem, nothing will ever happen to you. I will be next to you at every step along the way; anyone who ever thinks of harming you will be asking for a death wish." I whispered darkly as i tightened my hold on her before placing hot kisses down her throat, before leaning away to stare into her blue eyes.

Elizabeth looked at me before a smile made its way on her face. "You are so violent, you know that?"

I chuckled deeply as I gave her a squeeze and her words made me happy inside that she was starting to feel better.

"I never thought of hurting people so much until you came into my life." I shot back.

"Hey! Don't blame me for your violent tendencies." She smirked at me.

"But I do blame you." I murmured against her ear a I pulled her closer to me.

She looked deep in thought and I knew that she was thinking about the news.

"Is the fact that you are carrying my child makes you so sad?" I asked , frowning at her, I was afraid her answer would be yes because I didn't know what I will do then.

Her eyes widened as she shook her head and nuzzled my furiously. "No silly! It is just almost everyday there is a problem and I am not sure how we can raise a child at a time like this."

I didn't release I was holding my breath, anxious for her answer. I signed in relief at what she said.

"I will keep you safe...." I trailed off before I continued firmly, "You don't know you are my everything."

She gave me a smile and I could feel her smiling against my neck.

"I am happy we are having a child, Alex. I dreamt of it a quite few times." She told me softly as she blushed.

"Me too, since we completed the mating process." I told her sincerely as I brushed my lips against her hand.

"I have a small confession to make." I spoke up in a small voice.

"What is it?" she asked curiously.

Shifting in anxiety at her words, I cleared my throat. "I want a little girl; who looks just like you running around."

I smirked as she blushed and looked away. I always had that effect on her and I wouldn't want it any other way.

She moaned as I kissed her, but when I deepened the kiss she nimbly moved away from my grasp.

"I think the pack needs you now to talk about what happened." She said impishly.

She giggled when I scowled at her as I tried to adjust myself.

"I blame you for leaving me in a half-aroused state most of the time." I muttered and she laughed even louder.

I am glad she is laughing now. I was also glad that she accepted the pup because if she didn't I would probably be in a state of despair right now.

Grabbing her hand and placing my other hand on her belly, I made the three of us a promise which I vowed to keep.

I will keep you two always safe.

"What's the plan?" Drew asked and I could see he was trying to control his anger.

"We wipe them all." I growled as I glared murderously at the rogue they managed to catch during the fight.

He killed himself, before I could get the chance to do it myself.

"They went into hiding, we were unable to know their location." Drew's voice snapped me from my murderous thoughts as I glanced at him.

"You know they will come to me, he wants to kill me." I growled as I punched the wall. I wouldn't calm down until Elizabeth's father, John, is brought here and I could kill himself myself.

"That is why we must wait for them." Drew said slowly as if trying to make me understand.

I couldn't just wait till they strike, they may cause more deaths next time and I wouldn't allow that. It may hurt Elizabeth next time and I growled at the though. I wanted to find him quickly to keep the pack and Elizabeth safe.

I didn't want her to get hurt and I didn't want our child to be born in a place full of those people who killed people from other packs.

Drew was about to say something but was stopped by Leo's, my third in commend, arrival when he walked into the room. He was out of breath.

"Alpha.." He coughed before taking a few breaths.

"What?" I yelled at him to continue.

"I just saw the Luna and your sister leaving in a car." Not a second passed before I had him by the throat against the wall, baring my teeth at him.

"What do you mean by that?" I growled as I watched his eyes widen and he tried to compose himself.

"I was coming here and I saw them leaving. I tried to stop them but I was late." He said and with that last sentence I dropped him on the floor.

My mate with my sister; i I didn't like the thought of her going out without me or Drew but she is with my sister and for me, it was a dangerous to leave my mate with her.

That was it, I shifted to my black wolf and it dominated the whole place. Drew stood in my way but I snarled at him and I ran to the place where I now knew where my mate is.

I heard Drew's car behind me and I knew he was coming to stop me from doing a big damage but he wouldn't be able to stop me this time.

I am coming Elizabeth, just wait.

18

— ◦ —

CHAPTER 18

Elizabeth's POV

"Care to explain why you went with her, without so much as informing me?" He growled as he paced in front of me. He was pratically fumming and i couldn't think of a way to calm him down.

"She just wanted to talk, how can that be such a problem to you!" My tone raised a little till i was shouting at him now.

We have been having this argument for the past hour, I couldn't think of an excuse to why i went with her because if i did, making him calm down will be impossible.

"And what did you two talk about, if i may ask?" He snarled as his eyes turned the shade of black which made me anxious.

I looked anywhere but him at the moment.

If he knew the real reason, he would make sure Emma didn't step foot in the pack ever again. I couldn't allow that to happen, not after what she told me.

I opened my mouth to respond but i was silenced as Alex placed his hand on my mouth and slowly shook his head before whispering,

"No lying because i know when you are about to tell a lie." He told me slowly before removing his hand and towering over me.

"I-"

I felt the temperature of the room increase suddenly but it wasn't the weather, it was me being nervous and i hated it that he knew me so well.

He is your mate! he knows you so well to know when you lie My wolf reminded me and i mentally agreed with her.

"You know about Emma's mate now, don't you?" His tone was emtionless as he stared at me; studying my reaction.

I inhaled deeply before looking at the ground, I didn't know how to answer but he knew that i knew so what was the point of not talking about it.

"Yes, he was my half brother." I told him and i was the glad that my voice didn't crack.

Alex's face remained like a stone, without any emotion showing on his face but his eyes showed he was in deep thought.

"Yes, he is your half brother and i killed him and you already know why." He growled as he slammed his fist to the wall, making it crack.

I winced at the sound; he had the right to be angry. My half brother, which i had no idea he existed, killed Alex's parents and Alex, in return, killed him.

My half brother was Emma's mate and also The one who killed Alex's parents.

The news of his death didn't affect me at all, i didn't know he existed so it was normal for me not to feel anything.

"That is why your father wants to kill me; for revenge but i will kill him myself before he have the chance." Alex snarled, clenching his fist till his knuckles turned white.

It all made sence to me now, why my father's first goal now was to kill Alex and that thought didn't sit so well with me.

"I know and i believe in you." I told him softly before pecking him on the cheek.

However, he took that apportunity and slammed his lips on mine and i moaned loudly, running my hands through his hair. He pulled away quickly and i pouted before he smirked.

"I didn't know i was that desirable to you." He said smirking at me as i blushed.

"Idiot." I muttered lowly but he heard.

"You misspelled sexy, amazing, incredible and irresistable." He told me as he smiled confidently to himself and i chuckled at his attempt to light the situation.

"I just don't want you angry with me when i am finished with your father." He said sharply as he looked down at me.

"You are my mate and he wants to kill you so you know what you have to do; just be careful." I smiled reassuringly.

I would be sad over my father but he had done so many terrible things that someone had to put an end to it.

I just didn't know the person to do it will be my mate.

"Good morning sleepyhead." A voice said, a bit too loudly for my liking.

I groaned as i sat up and instantly shielded my eyes from the curtains. I turned around to glare at Alex but it wasn't him next to me.

It was Drew.

"Get out of the room." I snapped as i pointef towards the door. I knew it was childish but i was still angry at him and i don't think i was ready to forgive him yet.

"Not happening and also it is 2 PM, did you stay up late for a certain reason?" He smirked as he raised his eyebrows suggestively.

I blushed as i looked away from him, it wasn't his buisness to know what i and Alex had done last night and i frowned at him.

"You really don't want to hear the answer." I told him, crossing my arms over my chest.

Drew coughed a few times and looked away and i almost laughed at his reaction.

"Fine! i don't want to know but i just came here to say i am sorry for the way i acted towards you. It was wrong of me to tell you these things but i was worried about you and Lucy." He said as he looked at me and i could say he was sincere about it.

"You were worried about me and Lucy, is that the only reason?" I asked as i raised an eyebrow at him and a smirk formed on my lips as i saw him gulp in nervousness.

"Well that and you know that Alex will kill me if anything happens to you while i was there." He said as he now glared at me as if it was my fault.

"I still don't know if i can forg-" I was interrupted by him rasing his hands.

"Forgive me and i will take you to the mall, what do you say?" He told me, laughing at me as i quickly nodded.

"What about Alex?" I said slowly as i didn't want Alex hitting Drew because of me.

"He won't return till 6 PM and i guess we can go and return before it." He told me as if it is that easy which i knew wasn't.

I immediately got up from the bed and rushed to the bathroom but was stopped by a hand wrapping aroung my wrist.

"You are pregnant, congratulations!" He smiled as he pulled me for a hug. He noticed i was stiff because he pulled away.

"What's wrong?" His tone was full of concern.

"How did you know?" I asked, confusion was clear in my voice as i waited for him to answer.

"All the pack knows." He said slowly as if i was missing something. I grew irrated as i didn't understand anything.

"What do you mean all the pack knows exactly?" I hissed as i narrowed my eyes at him.

"Alex mind linked all the pack members about it, he didn't tell you?" He asked even though he knew the answer from my expression.

How can Alex tell all the pack without telling me he was going to do first! I wanted him to ask me if he could before it, it is too late now

"Are you okay?" Drew's voice snapped me back to reality and i took a few breaths to calm down.

"Yes! Let's not waste anymore time, shall we?" I smiled as i entered the bathroom and slammed the door so loudly, i was glad it didn't break.

I grinned as a thought came to me to get back at Alex.

Two can play this game Alex.

CHAPTER 19

"You will be the death of me, literally." Drew groaned behind me for the hunderdth time since we came here. I rolled my eyes and continued looking at the shops, I realised it has been a long time since i came here.

"Stop being a coward! you shouldn't be so afraid of Alex." I told him as i glared at nothing in practiculer as i remembered what Alex did.

"I just fear for my life so don't blame me!" He huffed as he walked beside me. I could feel he was irrated and i giggled.

"Why are you laughing?" He snapped as he crossed his arms over his chest and glared at me.

"Drew, you are a joke when it comes to being afraid of Alex." I chuckled as i wipped my imaginary tears.

He rolled his eyes and shook his head at me.

"You are evil, you know that?" He smiled for the first time since we came here.

"Only with you." I laughed at his schocked expression and strode away quickly.

A dress suddenly caught my eyes and i hurried to the store to take a good look at it but the person who was inside made me gasp. I double checked if I was correct but here she was standing.

Emma

She was talking to a man whom i had never seen before. He wasn't from the pack, i was sure of that and i knew he was a rogue.

Why would there be a rogue in the pack and emma talking to him

Too many thoughts ran through my mind as i watched them, they looked really engrossed in the conversation.

"Here you ar-" I put my hand on Drew's mouth quickly and motioned for him to keep quiet.

He raised an eyebrow but i only pointed at Emma and the rogue.

Do you know him? I mindlinked Drew but he shook his head and his eyes turned to a darker shade of blue and he clenshed his fists.

A rogue, I will go see what is there. Stay here.He said before he made a move to get up but i held his hand and shook my head at him.

Whatever they are talking about is a secret, they will stop talking as soon as they notice we are here. I have an idea. I mindlinked him back. Before he could protest, I stood up and moved as closely to them as i could; trying not to get noticed in the process.

Thanks to my hearing abilities, i could make up some of their words.

"So your brother is going to war soon." The man said in a commending voice.

"Yes, he is making sure everything is ready. I don't know when he will start but it is soon." Emma replied.

I gasped as i covered my mouth. She was betraying Alex, I suspected there was something else to the story but it was clear that she was betraying the pack right now.

"We will be sure to elimante his pack as soon as we can starting with the luna." He growled as his eyes turned midnight black.

I gulped as i heard this, he was talking about me and he looked serious about killing me.

I looked down and realized my hands were trembling, I wished Alex was with me now to see this.

I expected Emma to defend me or anything related to that but i couldn't be more wrong.

"Something is up with her these days, I don't know what but there is something. The alpha also seems more protective over her." She told him and i could feel she was happy to tell that man information about me.

I signed in relief knowing news about my pregnancy didn't reach her.

"I have to go now, I will let you know about the next move soon." He said and with that he turned and left the store, Emma following closely behind.

There was no way I am going to let them leave before knowing the whole story. I didn't know where the courage came from but i stood up and followed them, knowing that i could be hurt in the process.

I walked out of the store and searched for Drew but he was nowhere in sight. I frowned as i looking around me, fearing that the man did something to him.

"Looking for him?" A cold voice muttered behind me.

I whirled behind so quickly, ready to defend myself against the man but to my relief it was just Alex looking furious while holding Drew with his collar.

"Alex you have t-" I began to say but i was interrupted by him growling. I was surprised that people around us didn't notice.

"I told you to stay at home but you can't do anything I say, can you?!" He sneered, mocking me as he let Drew go and stormed towards me.

"Emma, she is w-" But i was interrupted again by him.

"You have been with her again! Didn't you get it when i told you to stay away from her, Stay Away from her!" Alex suddenly snapped as he crashed me to his chest and inhaled my scent, ensuring that I was okay.

I pushed him away, now angry that he can't just listen to me for one minute.

"Emma is betraying the whole pack! I saw her there talking to a rogue and telling them information about the pack." I took a deep breath after i finished, i didn't like talking about the betrayel of Emma; she was the only family member left for Alex.

Alex stared at me for a moment then he suddenly began laughing so loudly that it drew people's attention.

It was clear he didn't believe me, i suspected he wouldn't but i didn't expect this reaction.

"I am not lying to you Alex, i swear i saw them there." I snapped at him, i couldn't take his laughing anymore. I didn't even know the joke in it.

"I am sorry Elizabeth but i knew that all along, you just found out a little late." He told me then smirked as if what he just said was no big deal.

"What?" It was the only word i could utter as i tried to process what Alex just said.

"I knew all along but i gave her false information about our pack so whatever she is telling the rogues is wrong." He told me but i didn't miss the sadness in his eyes at the mention of Emma betraying him.

"But why not stop her? why let her tell rogues about us?" I asked even though i already knew the answer.

"She tells then information and in turn they tell her information, i have people from the pack watching her and they report everything she does to me." He told me and he stood there regarding me.

I was shocked and even hurt that Alex didn't tell me earlier. I was stupid for not seeing it earlier, Alex warning me to stay away from her and Alex killing her mate; it was clear she wanted revenge.

A hand carressed my check softly and i leaned into it, seeking comfort.

"I am sorry i didn't tell you earlier, i didn't want to stress you anymore. You are pregnant and I don't want you to worry about things like this when i can handle them myself." He whispered softly in my ear.

His words made sense but i didn't want to be kept in the dark all the time.

"Promise me you won't hide anything from me again." I said but before he could protest I continued, "If you don't i will find out on my own and that means getting out of the house without you knowing."

His eyes turned to that dark shade I am used to now and I knew he was deciding, he looked in deep thought but I already knew what the answer would me.

"Fine but you will listen to anything i have to say now." He growled and he looked dead serious about it.

I nodded and that action alone seemed to calm him down.

"Come on, let's go to the pack house." He said, taking my hands and making me follow him.

Drew came behind us but Alex stopped him.

"Enjoy your beta title because i don't think you will have it for long, that is a promise." Alex sneered at him and with that, He took my hand and tugged me behind him.

I cast a look at Drew to see him glaring at me. I mouthed the word sorry but he just ignored me and continued walking.

I smiled since I knew he won't remain angry at me for so long, not when i am planning to make his favourite meal tomorrow for lunch.

Knowing how much Drew loves food, i knew he would forgive me in an instant.

We arrived to the pack house in half an hour. Once we arrived, people from the pack hurried to the car.

Alex got up quickly and ran towards the pack house, I got out and hurried after him but once i reached him, he pulled me behind his back.

And that is when i saw it there were 2 bodies on the ground, they were almost unrecognizable because there was so much blood on their faces.

It was a man and woman and they were killed in a brutal way, that was obvious.

I felt tears running down my checks at the scene infront of me. Who could have entered the pack and killed them without people taking notice.

There was a piece of paper on the woman's lap and Alex picked it up and unfolded it.

His body suddenly shook and he growled so loudly that i felt shivers run down my spine and i am sure all the people from the pack did feel it. By now his teeth were bared and veins bulged from his bare arms.

I picked up the paper and my eyes widned as i read what is writtern in the paper.

Your mate will be next, war is sooner that you think.

20

CHAPTER 20

The following days passed so quickly, that I had no idea of what's actually going on. People of the pack were always in the pack house, making plans for attacking my father's pack which we had no idea their whereabouts right now; only that there were attacks here and there and werewolfs getting kidnapped.

My father was building a bigger group, to destroy Alex's pack.

Alex was a mess, he wasn't his usual self. He somehow got angrier on any person in the pack who dared to go against his orders. The pack fighters trained every day now and of course Alex got more protective over me.

I wasn't allowed to leave the house at all, I couldn't take being in the house any longer but I saw the stress he was under and I couldn't add to it so I kept quiet and tried to help in anything I could which wasn't a lot seeing that I am pregnant and Alex wouldn't have me do anything in the pack.

"You have any other idea?" Drew's voice startled me from my thoughts. He didn't look carefree as he used to, he no longer made jokes here and there, he kept me company in the house when he wasn't helping Alex which was most of the time.

"I don't know, give her some time." I muttered as I looked out of the window where Alex was talking to a pack fighter, he looked angry but he was like this all the time since the attack that happened.

"You know I can't, not when I am going to this war and may never come back." He shot back before taking a few breaths.

Did I mention that Drew became like Alex in getting angry most of the time?

I quickly moved towards him and wrapped my arms around him. I felt something wet slide against my cheek and released that I was crying. It wasn't the first time but I always cried when I was alone.

I was terrified that pack fighters, Drew and Alex wouldn't come back. I knew deep inside that if anything happened to Alex in this war, I wouldn't be able to live with myself anymore.

"Don't say that, you will be fine. You are Drew after all." I pulled back and smirked at him. He gave a small smile before wiping my cheek with his finger.

"It is just that I want to show her that I love her but she only seems to ignore me since.." Drew stopped and looked away.

I giggled as I remembered what happened. Some girl came and told Lucy about Drew's reputation as a play boy and his history with girls. Why the girl did that? Well, Drew broke her heart in high school, apparently she never did get over it and wanted revenge.

I tried to convince Lucy that Drew stopped all that once he found out he was her mate and that was all in the past but she still can't get over it.

For the past hour, Drew and I have been thinking of ideas to make Lucy forgive him but all suggestions seemed useless.

"Take her out for a walk and beg for her forgiveness, Arrange a romantic date for her; I am sure she will love that." I told him, feeling pretty happy with this.

"Sounds nice and maybe I could sing a song for her, I have been thinking about it for some time." He replied, sounding deep in thought.

"What song? Do you even know how to choose a nice song?" I frowned at him.

"Leave it to the luna who has no taste in music." He rolled his eyes at me and laughed as I narrowed my eyes at him.

"what song are you thinking about then, impress me." I shot back as I challenged him.

"Fine but after it you will wish Alex could do something like this for you." His eyes serious. I was about to replay but stopped once he began.

"Your hand fits in mine, like its made just for me, but bear this in mind, It was meant to be, and I'm joining up the dots, with the freckles on your cheeks, and it all makes sense to me, I know you've never loved, the crinkles by your eyes, when you smile, you've never loved, Your stomach or your thighs, the dimples in your back, at the bottom of your spine, but I love them endlessly, I wont let these little things, slip out of my mouth, but if I do, It's you, oh it's you, they add up to, I'm in love with you, and all these little things"

I never knew Drew had such a wonderful voice, I was about to tell him that it was so good if it weren't for the clapping behind me. I turned around so quickly and was surprised to see Alex there, grinning at Drew.

"You know Drew, You would be a better singer than a beta." Alex smirked at him but was rewarded with a laugh from me and a frown from Drew.

"Says the person who would fit better in horror movies than being an Alpha." Drew shot back as he crossed his hands over his chest.

"You better apply for a job because I feel your position as a beta won't last long." Alex replied, smirking.

Drew just glared at him before looking at me and completely ignoring Alex.

"What do you think?" He asked with that hopeful look, I smiled at him.

"Your voice is amazing and I am sure Lucy will forgive you in an instant after hearing this." I replied.

"It wasn't bad." Alex told him, cracking a real smile.

"I never asked for your opinion, Alex." Drew smirked but was wise to leave to the room quickly when Alex growled at him.

I actually enjoyed their silly arguments, I can totally see that they were childhood best friends.

"What are you smiling at?" Alex asked softly as he sat down and put me on his lap.

"Just you and Drew." I replied as I ran my hands through his hair. He looked really stressed and I blamed my father for all the things he put Alex through.

"I don't know why do you like him so much." He mocked as he nuzzled my neck and I sighed happily.

It has been a while since Alex was like this and I relished every moment in it.

But something was off about him, there was something on his mind; that was clear.

"Alex what is there and don't you dare say it is nothing because you will be lying." I said, my eyes serious as I stared at him.

"We know the location of your father, I am leaving after 3 days." Alex sighed again and hugged me closer.

A foreboding feeling began to swell in my chest. A feeling that something bad and painful was about to occur. Panic began to rise within me, but I quickly pushed it down.

"Alright. Let me get my things ready," I said, trying to keep my voice from trembling.

I rose from the bed, but Alex grabbed my waist and pulled me back down before I could set my feet on the floor.

"I'm going. You're staying. You are pregnant or have you forgotten," he told me firmly.

"What?!" I practically yelled. "I'm coming with you whether you like it or not, I know I am pregnant but I can't sit here; wondering whether you are hurt or not" I told him defiantly, trying to stand up. "Now let me go!"

Alex smirked inwardly but kept his hold on me.

"Elizabeth, please try to understand," he told me softly, "but I will be too busy fighting and leading an army to keep an eye on you." He lifted my chin so I could meet his eyes, "I will never forgive myself if something happened to you or the pup." He continued, placing his hand on my stomach.

I touched his cheek.

"But, Alex, what if you got injured or something?" I said softly, "Then I won't be able to be able to help you."

Alex gave me a small smile.

"Don't worry. Did you forget I'm an Alpha? Nothing can touch me. Well, except for you of course," he added with a grin.

I blushed lightly.

"Alex, stop it," I said and lightly slapped his chest, "This is serious, what if you don't come back? What if you get...killed? Then what will I do?" I asked him.

"Love, I promise I won't get myself killed. Haven't I shown you that I never give up? It would probably only take a few days, perhaps a bit more to defeat them. I'll be back before you know it," he tried to reassure me, stroking my back caringly.

But I was not satisfied. That strange, painful feeling still clung to my heart, making it slightly difficult for me to breathe normally.

"Promise you'll come back to me alive and well. Promise you'll return. Alex, promise me," I pleaded urgently as I gripped his shirt.

Cupping each side of my face tenderly with his strong, pale hands, Alex looked deep into my eyes.

"Elizabeth, I promise you with everything that I am that I will come back to you. Even if I have to swim an entire ocean, even if I have to kill the entire Rogue army by myself, I promise you that I would do the impossible to return to your arms in order to keep loving you always."

I flung myself into his arms, hugging his middle tightly.

"Beth I love you." he said fervently against my lips.

"And I love you, Alex," I whispered back as I held onto him as if afraid I would lose him the instant I let go.

Gently easing me onto my back, Alex slowly untied the sash that held my blue dress closed. He pulled away from their kiss and opened my robe to reveal my exposed breasts.

Alex cocked his eyebrow at his me.

"You were waiting for me weren't you, love?" he purred.

I grinned as I laced one of her hands behind his neck while the other snaked its way to his hard length that was poking at my thigh.

I then seductively replied, "Just like I will be when you return from the war."

I squeezed his manhood, causing him to groan heatedly.

Alex growled lowly as he attacked my neck with searing kisses.

2 days passed so quickly and I cried most of the time, blame it on my hormones. I didn't want Alex to leave; I was afraid he wouldn't come back. He reassured numerous times but I still was worried.

We were currently at the pack doctor's house, Alex insisted that I must go to make sure that me and the pup were okay and of course he came with me. His happiness made me smile a little but I didn't feel okay, knowing he would be leaving soon.

After making sure I and the baby were okay, we left but Alex has this weird looking bottle in his hand.

"What's this?" I asked, pointing at the bottle.

"I know you have been stressed over everything the last few days, so I ordered for this to be brought to you to lessen the stress. I am sorry it was late but he had to travel to the neighboring pack to bring and inspect it."Alex replied, smiling at me.

"I don't know how to thank you." I smiled as I meant every word. He was too good for me.

"You well being is enough for me." He told me, handing me the bottle.

I opened it and smelled the liquid inside it, it smelled weird but it was to lessen the stress so I really needed it.

I swallowed some of it and I almost puked everything I have eaten; its taste was horrible.

Everything happened so quickly after that, I had fallen down on the floor so quickly that at first I had been too stunned to think or speak, much less move. I lay there with the side of my face pressed to the ground, unable to breathe for several seconds. After I caught my breath and wiggled both my fingers and toes, I felt Alex holding me as I heard him yelling, And then a stabbing pain shot through my lower abdomen, and already I knew what was happening, I saw the unmistakable sight of blood.

There was no mistaking the voice of Alex's growling at my side, people around us ran towards me but I couldn't concentrate on anything around me.

The liquid inside the bottle wasn't to lessen my stress, it was a poison to kill my baby. I faintly heard people shouting, before everything went black.

21

EPILOGUE

I woke up feeling disorientated. My mind was foggy and I couldn't open my eyes; Alex's scent was all over the room, the scent that always brought me comfort; now couldn't.

My baby

Tears ran down my cheeks involuntary and I tried to wipe them but couldn't. More tears kept falling. I felt the bed shift under me and Alex bringing me over his lap and wrapping his arms around me.

He kissed my cheek and whispered comforting words in my ears but it didn't have an effect on me.

"hush, rest. You are okay." Alex whispered in my ears but I shook my head before finally managing to open my arms.

"What about the baby?" I didn't to ask, I already know the answer but I felt I had to.

"The baby was just 6 weeks along, it was still small." Alex swallowed before looking away.

The lack of emotions in his voice in his voice and how his body shook broke my heart to see him like this. I finally looked at his and found his eyes looking red; he was crying when I was asleep. It was obvious.

"What happened?" I whispered as I had no idea what happened. The last thing I remember was taking the bottle Alex gave me and then I fainted.

"The bottle that I gave you, it contained poison; made to kill the baby." He said harshly and clenched his fist as he remembered what happened.

"But the doctor-" I began to say but was cut off quickly by Alex who shook his head.

"He betrayed the pack and put the poison in the bottle." He said harshly, his voice promising death to the doctor.

"Why?" I asked, the tears returned to my eyes easily, even though I had tried to clear them to not add to Alex's sadness.

"Your father had his mate kidnapped and he told him to put the poison or his mate will be killed." Alex growled, his voice made me shrink back a little.

I didn't need to ask but I already know that Alex killed the doctor and I didn't feel remorse in it. The doctor had to do it but I am sure there must have been a way to warn Alex before it happened.

"Alex, I am not angry at you because you killed him." I said, managing a small smile. I wanted to make him feel better. I was miserable from the inside; nothing was going to make me feel better expect one thing.

To kill the person responsible for my baby's death

"I wouldn't have cared if you were anyway." He said coldly, looking at me with his eyes which have turned to an unbelievably a darker shade.

I decided something. I know Alex was going to kill my father but I didn't want him to. I wanted to do it myself. There was a fire burning inside me which wouldn't calm down until I do this.

I may have lost the baby and I may still be weak but I will go with Alex to the war to fight side by side with him and I will be the one to kill their leader, my father.

Revenge was never a good thing, I know it but I didn't care right now, the only thing running through my mind was getting my revenge and I don't care if Alex refused because I was going with him whether he liked it or not.

"I am sorry." Alex said after minutes of silence, running his hand through my hair.

"For what?" I asked, confused as to why he was apologizing now. It was his fault, it was my father's fault.

"Because I gave it to you, if I didn't the pup would still-" then he just broke down. Heaving sobs left his chest.

It wasn't his fault, it was never his and I know he was trying to put the blame on himself. I knew long ago that Alex has made his mission to protect me and if anything happened to me and he had nothing to do with it, he would still blame himself.

I kissed him softly on the lips and it seemed to calm him down a little. I pulled away before whispering in his ears. "It isn't your fault and you know it. Don't waste time and lets kill the person who is to blame for this."

Alex looked at me seriously before smirking. "You aren't coming and you know it." His voice was hard and strong. I was about to protest but the edge of his tone angered her.

"I am coming whether you agree or not. It was our baby who died Alex, not just yours and I have the right to come with you." I declared, turning away from Alex.

He grabbed my chin and turned me around to face him, he stared into my eyes before sighing.

"I will let you come with me, only because you will never be okay if I didn't let you come. You are mate, my heart will always belong to you. I won't let anything harm you and I promise you this will be the last time you will get hurt." Then he kissed me so slowly and softly that I know he meant every word.

I loved him as much he loved him and I intended for both of us to take my father's army and have our happily ever after.

Reluctantly, he broke the kiss, rubbing my cheek as he stared down at me. My heart was pounding now.

"Thank you for letting me come with you and I promise I will never let anyone hurt me." I said, smiling for the first time now.

"Sleep then, love. We have a long journey tomorrow." His voice resolute as he laid me down on the bed and laid beside me.

"I love you Alex." I said before yawning. I was really tired and the best solution was to sleep because starting from tomorrow, I am sure there will be no rest.

"I love you too and I came to terms that I will always love you more." He said softly in my ears before nuzzling my neck.

I just smiled at what he said, He thinks he loves me more but he was so wrong.

"Now sleep." His said softly as he kissed my cheek and ran his hand along my back.

He didn't need to say it again because sleep came to me quickly and I slept in the comfort of Alex's arms.